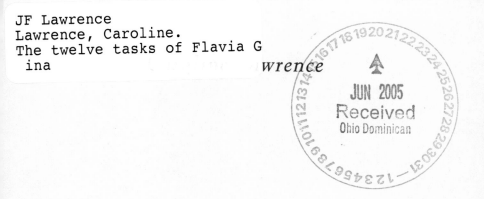

*The Roman Mysteries: Book VI*

# THE TWELVE TASKS
# OF FLAVIA GEMINA

ROARING BROOK PRESS
Brookfield, Connecticut

Copyright © 2003 by Caroline Lawrence
Published by Roaring Brook Press
Roaring Brook Press is a division of Holtzbrinck Publishing Holdings Limited Partnership
2 Old New Milford Road, Brookfield, Connecticut 06804.
First published in the United Kingdom in 2003 by Orion Children's Books, London
Maps by Richard Russell Lawrence copyright © 2003 by Orion Children's Books.

Distributed in Canada by H. B. Fenn and Company Ltd.

Library of Congress Cataloging-in-Publication Data
Lawrence, Caroline.
The twelve tasks of Flavia Gemina / Caroline Lawrence.
p. cm.—(The Roman mysteries ; bk. 6)
Summary: When a Roman widow shows unusual interest in Flavia's father,
Flavia decides to discover Cartila's true motives by performing twelve tasks,
just like the Greek hero Hercules.
[1. Stepmothers—Fiction. 2. Rome—History—Empire, 30 B.C.-476 A.D.—Fiction.
3. Sex role—Fiction. 4. Mystery and detective stories.]   I. Title.
PZ7.L425Twe 2004        [Fic]—dc22
2003027798
ISBN: 1-59643-012-5

Roaring Brook Press books are available for special promotions and premiums.
For details contact: Director of Special Markets, Holtzbrinck Publishers.

First American Edition October 2003
Printed in the United States of America
2   4   6   8   10   9   7   5   3   1

*To my sister, Jennifer*
*Who loves wisely and well*

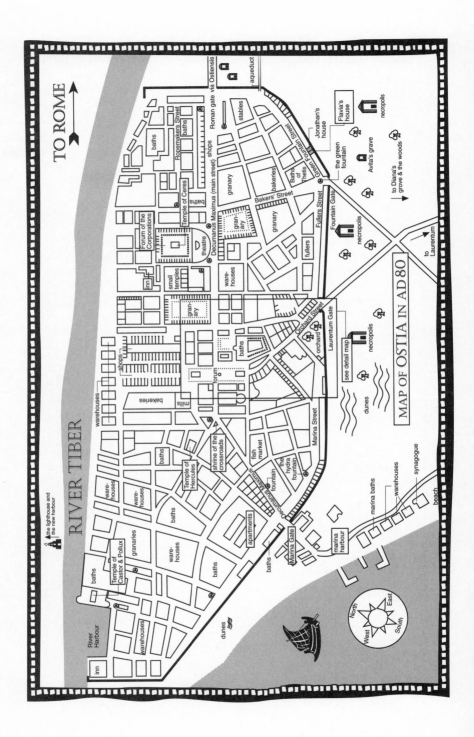

TO ROME

RIVER TIBER

the lighthouse and the new harbour

River Harbour

inn

baths

Temple of Castor & Pollux

granaries

ware-houses

ware-houses

warehouses

warehouses

baths

baths

Temple of Hercules

baths

dunes

apartments

shrine of the crossroads

fountain

fish market

the hydra fountain

Marina Gate

baths

marina harbour

marina baths

warehouses

synagogue

beach

warehouses

bakeries

mills

shops

forum

theatre

gran-ary

small temples

inn

Forum of the Corporations

Temple of Ceres

baths

baths

Ropemakers Street

baths

warehouses

baths

granary

theatre

Decumanus Maximus (main street)

Marina Street

Orchard Street

orchard

baths

see detail map

Laurentum Gate

necropolis

dunes

granary

granary

granary

bakeries

Bakers' Street

fullers

Fullers Street

Fountain Gate

necropolis

Baths of Thetis

Green Fountain Street

the green fountain

Jonathan's house

Avita's grave

to Diana's grove & the woods

Flavia's house

necropolis

Roman gate via Ostiensis

shops

stables

aqueduct

to Laurentum

MAP OF OSTIA IN AD 80

North
West
East
South

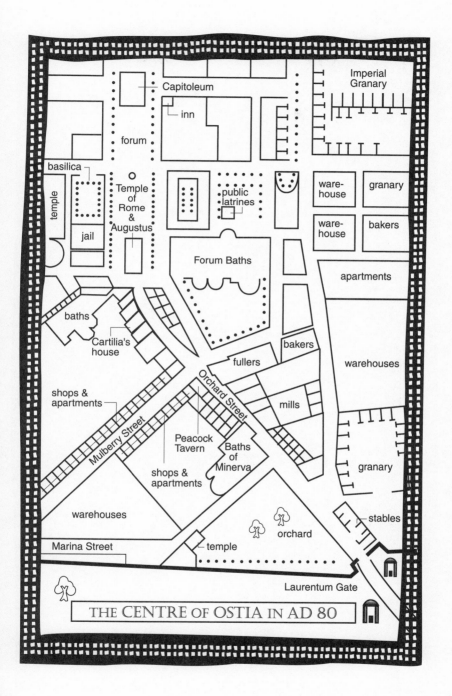

THE CENTRE OF OSTIA IN AD 80

Imperial Granary

Capitoleum

inn

forum

basilica

temple

Temple of Rome & Augustus

jail

public latrines

warehouse

granary

warehouse

bakers

apartments

Forum Baths

baths

Cartilia's house

bakers

fullers

warehouses

shops & apartments

Orchard Street

mills

Mulberry Street

Peacock Tavern

Baths of Minerva

shops & apartments

granary

stables

warehouses

Marina Street

temple

orchard

Laurentum Gate

# SCROLL I

The day Flavia Gemina learned she was to be married began like any other winter day in the Roman port of Ostia.

When Flavia awoke, shortly after dawn, the sky showed as pearly pink diamonds through the latticework screen of her window. She could hear rain gurgling in the gutters and there was a delicious freshness in the air: the smell of rich earth and wet brick. Flavia snuggled deeper under her woolen blanket and wormed her feet beneath her dog Scuto's warm bulk. Today was the day of her uncle's betrothal feast and tomorrow they were preparing for the festival of the Saturnalia, which would last five days. So there would be no lessons for a whole week.

Presently, the scent of spiced wine and scalded milk brought Flavia padding downstairs to the kitchen, her blanket wrapped round her. Scuto trailed behind, tail wagging absently.

"Good morning, dear," said Flavia's old nurse Alma, pouring hot milk into a ceramic cup half-filled with spiced wine. "Cheese or barley?"

"Both, please," said Flavia. "And a little pepper. Does pater have his poculum yet?"

"Yes," said Alma, sprinkling cheese and barley onto the steaming liquid. "I took it to him a few moments ago." She passed a cube of cheese over a silver grater so that melting curls covered the surface of the drink.

1

"There you are, my dear." Alma handed the poculum to Flavia.

"Thanks," murmured Flavia and sipped the warming drink. She ate some of the cheese-coated barley floating on top and reflected that she liked a drink she could chew. The barley made her think of Pistor the baker. She and her friends had spent most of November trying to discover who had been stealing his poppy seed rolls. Flavia liked mysteries, and in solving Pistor's case she had proved to herself that she really was a detective.

Her blanket still trailing behind, Flavia took her spiced drink out of the kitchen and along the peristyle to her father's study. On the other side of the red-based columns, rain fell softly on the inner garden. The fig tree had lost its leaves but the shrubs nodded under the rain's caress. Scuto wandered over to the quince bush to perform his morning ablutions.

"Morning, Caudex."

"Morning, Miss Flavia." The big door-slave was standing on a small wooden stool, winding spirals of glossy ivy round the columns.

"That looks nice." Flavia nodded her approval.

Caudex grunted.

On this mid-December day the rooms of the house were dimmer than usual. But in the study, a standing oil lamp added its golden glow to the pearly light filtering in from the garden. Beside the lamp was a copper brazier filled with glowing coals.

"Morning, pater."

"Good morning, my little owl." Marcus Flavius Geminus sat hunched over his desk, his toga draped round his shoulders like a blanket. He shot her a fond but distracted smile.

Flavia curled up on the old leather chair, tucking her feet up and pulling her blanket around her. For a moment she warmed her hands on the cup as she watched her father work.

She was still not used to his short hair. Two months ago the doctor had cut off his matted, lice-ridden locks, but at that time her

2

father had been too weak to dedicate his hair to the sea god. So last week he had shaved off the new growth and offered it at the Temple of Neptune to thank the god for sparing his life in a shipwreck. Now, his short hair and the new lines on his forehead made him look older. His face reminded Flavia of her grandfather's death mask in the household shrine.

Next door in the atrium, she could hear the rain gushing from lion-mouthed terra-cotta gutters and splashing into the pool beneath the skylight. From upstairs drifted the sound of flute and lyre. Flavia's ex-slave girl Nubia and their tutor Aristo practiced together every morning before breakfast. Aristo said he found it easiest to compose music straight after waking.

Scuto padded into the study from the garden, leaving wet paw-prints on the marble veneer floor. He sighed and sank heavily beneath the brazier. Soon the comforting smell of wet dog filled the room. It occurred to Flavia that, like her father, Scuto was also getting old.

"Pater?" Flavia took another sip of her hot spiced drink.

"Yes, sweetheart," he said absently, his head bent over a papyrus tally sheet.

"Pater, have the sands of time just about run out for you?"

He gave her an amused glance. "I'm only thirty-one," he said. "I trust I have a few years left." He looked back at his sums and frowned.

"Pater?"

"Yes, Flavia?"

"Pater, are we poor now?"

Her father sighed and put down his quill pen and turned to face her.

"I mean," said Flavia, "they won't take our house away, will they?"

"No, my little owl. They won't take the house away. A gift from an anonymous benefactor saved our house."

Flavia nodded. Her father still didn't know that she herself was the unknown donor.

"As for our daily living expenses," he said, "I may have to sell the divine Vespasian. Titus, too."

"Oh no!" said Flavia, looking at the marble busts of the current emperor and his scowling father. "I like them. I like things just the way they are. Don't change anything."

He sighed. "My only other option is to ask my patron Cordius to lend us enough money to see us through the winter." Her father shook his head. "Usually at this time of year I've plenty of cash on deposit with my bankers. But I'd invested everything in that cargo of spices and when it went down with the *Myrtilla* . . ." His voice trailed off and he stared down at the sheets on his desk.

Flavia could guess what he was thinking. Her father had named his ship after Flavia's mother, Myrtilla, who had died in childbirth seven years previously. Now he had lost both Myrtillas.

"But you can use the ship Lupus inherited, can't you?" said Flavia in her brightest voice.

"Yes." Her father smiled. "But the *Delphina* needs some work done to her before the sailing season begins. And we'll need to perform the purification ceremony. That means purchasing a bull: another vast expense." Her father's chair scraped on the marble veneer floor as he pushed it back. "Flavia." He stood.

"Yes, pater?"

"Flavia, you must be very discreet. You must not let anyone know that we are in debt. If people know we're struggling financially, they'll take advantage of us. I may even be stripped of my rank as an equestrian. We must behave as if we are prosperous, but without spending anything more than is absolutely necessary." Her father tugged at the folds of his toga to make them hang properly over his shoulder.

"I understand, Pater," said Flavia with a sigh. She had been planning to ask him for money to buy Saturnalia gifts for her friends, but now that looked impossible.

4

Her face brightened as Nubia appeared in the doorway, holding a steaming cup.

"Good morning, Nubia!"

"Good morning, Flavia." Nubia sipped her drink and watched her puppy Nipur romp into the study. He was pure black, almost as big as Scuto and still growing. He greeted Flavia and her father with wagging tail and acknowledged Scuto with a brief sniff. Then he hurried back into the garden to see if the rain had brought out any snails.

A young man appeared beside Nubia in the wide doorway. Their tutor Aristo was a handsome Greek with intelligent brown eyes and curly hair the color of dark bronze. Today he was wearing a thick, oatmeal-colored tunic, leather boots, and a short red cape. A net was slung over his left shoulder and in his right hand he held a light spear.

"I'm just off hunting," he said. "I'll be back in time for . . ." He took a deep breath. "I'll be back by the seventh hour."

Captain Geminus gave Aristo a grateful look. "May Diana give you luck with the hunt," he said. "I believe we ate the last of your friend's quail pie yesterday afternoon."

"I'll try to catch us a big boar for the Saturnalia." Aristo disappeared toward the back door.

"I'm off now, too," said Flavia's father. "Going to the barber and then to see my patron Cordius. I'll be back in a few hours. Oh, Flavia. Hercules the wall painter is coming today to make a start on the new fresco in the dining room."

"A wall painter? I thought you said we had to be careful with our money."

"He's doing it *gratis*. He owes me a favor," said Flavia's father, and added, "I gave him free passage to Sicily last year. Besides, it will give the impression that we're well off. He doesn't celebrate the Saturnalia so he'll be working here over the next week."

"Imagine not celebrating the best festival of all," murmured Flavia.

"Good-bye, sweetheart." Flavia's father bent to kiss her forehead.

5

"Good-bye, Nubia." He disappeared into the atrium and a moment later Flavia heard the front door close and the bolt fall into place.

Nubia lingered in the peristyle, looking anxiously toward the back door. "I hope Aristo is joking," she said. "I hope there are no foaming boars in the woods today."

"He looked sad," remarked Flavia. "And the music you were playing was sad, too."

"I know. He is wretched because of today, because he is still loving Miriam." Nubia shivered.

Flavia opened her blanket. "Come and sit beside me, Nubia."

Nubia squeezed onto the chair and pulled her side of the blanket round. "It is most chilly," she said.

Flavia knew that Nubia was used to the dry desert heat, not damp Italian winters. And this winter was particularly damp and cold. Everyone blamed the weather on the volcano which had erupted at the end of August. Flavia's nurse Alma said it was just laziness: "They'll be blaming Vesuvius for everything that happens over the next twenty years," she had grumbled. "I've known colder winters."

But Nubia obviously hadn't. She was still shivering.

"You should wear more than one tunic," said Flavia, putting her arm round Nubia's shoulder and rubbing briskly. "Like the divine Emperor Augustus. He used to wear five tunics in the winter."

"Yes. I will do that."

"And we'll go to the baths later," promised Flavia. "After we've been to the market."

"Good," said Nubia. "I will sit in the steamy sudatorium."

A loud knocking on the front door brought Scuto to his feet and Nipur in from the garden. They skittered across the study and into the atrium.

Flavia heard Caudex grumbling in the peristyle, so she called out, "We'll get it, Caudex!"

Leaving the blanket on the chair, she and Nubia went into the atrium and past the rainwater pool to the oak door with its heavy bolt. Scuto and Nipur were scrabbling at the wood. They could smell their friend Tigris on the other side.

The door swung open to reveal two boys and a puppy standing in the shelter of the porch. They were dripping wet and their breath came in excited white puffs.

"Just come from shopping in the forum. . . ." Jonathan, the taller of the two, suffered from asthma. "You'll never guess . . . what happened!" he gasped. "The whole town is . . . talking about it! Ship from Alexandria . . . delayed by storms . . . carrying animals for the games. . . ."

Lupus—the younger boy—was making marks on a tablet, nodding as he wrote. He had no tongue and a wax tablet was his main form of communication.

"Animals. . . ." Jonathan was leaning on the door frame. "Wild, ravenous beasts . . . the lion knocked the trainer . . . off the gangplank and . . . all the animals escaped!"

"A lion?" breathed Flavia. She and Nubia exchanged wide-eyed looks.

"Other animals, too. . . ." Jonathan was still breathless.

"What animals?" asked Nubia.

"You tell them, Lupus," gasped Jonathan.

This was the moment Lupus had been waiting for. He held up his wax tablet and Flavia squealed as she read what he had written:

# ESCAPED ANIMALS!!!
# LION
# CAMELOPARD
# ELEPHANT
# AND A GIANT MAN-EATING BIRD!!!

# SCROLL II

"A giant man-eating bird?" cried Flavia. "Like the Stymphalian bird Hercules had to kill in the myth?"

Lupus nodded emphatically. One of his eyes was slightly bloodshot.

"Did you behold it?" Nubia asked.

"No," said Jonathan, stepping into the atrium. "But Decimus the scroll seller's son did. He said the bird was twice as big as a man, with a huge body, a long neck, and evil yellow eyes."

Lupus followed Jonathan into the atrium and bared his teeth fiercely.

"Oh, yes," said Jonathan, "and lots of sharp teeth!"

"A bird is having teeth?" said Nubia.

Jonathan shrugged. "According to Decimus."

"Have they caught any of the animals yet?" asked Flavia. She closed the door and made sure the bolt was down.

"No," said Jonathan. "That's why we came straight here. To warn you not to walk the dogs or go gathering ivy like yesterday. Apparently the elephant headed straight down the Decumanus Maximus toward Rome but the other animals ran along the beach toward the synagogue. They may have reached Laurentum by now. Or maybe they're hiding in the woods."

"Oh, I wish I'd seen the elephant running down the main street!" said Flavia.

"Aristo!" cried Nubia. Her fingers were digging into Flavia's arm.

"What about him?" said Jonathan.

"He is hunting," said Nubia. "In the woods."

"And all he has to protect himself," cried Flavia, "is a javelin and a net!"

Nubia's eyes were as round as gold coins. "We must warn him!"

"Are you crazy?" said Jonathan. "A bird as big as Ostia's lighthouse and a man-eating lion and a camelopard . . ."

"What is a camelopard, anyway?" asked Flavia, leading them along the corridor toward the kitchen.

Lupus shrugged and Jonathan said: "I don't know. I thought you might."

"We'd better look it up in Pliny's *Natural History*," said Flavia. "But first, do you two want a hot poculum?"

The boys nodded and followed her into the kitchen.

"Alma!" said Flavia. "There are some wild animals loose in the woods. They ran off a ship this morning!"

"Oh dear, oh dear," Alma tutted. "Not the first time that's happened. You'd better not go into the woods today. Barley or cheese for you, Wolfie?"

Lupus shook his head. Although the name Lupus meant "wolf," Alma was the only person he allowed to call him "Wolfie."

The friends lingered in the small kitchen, unwilling to leave the warmth of the glowing hearth. Alma didn't seem to mind. As the boys sipped their drinks, she turned back to her mortarium and continued grinding chestnuts into flour.

"So tell us what happened again," said Flavia. "How did the animals escape?"

Jonathan put his cup down and wiped a cheesy pink mustache from his upper lip. "Well, they think the ship from Alexandria was delayed by storms. Everyone was amazed to see a ship sail into the harbor in December. They must have run out of food. Decimus said the animals were ravenous."

9

Lupus roared.

"Yes," said Jonathan. "Decimus and his father were just setting up their bookstall in the forum when they heard this enormous roar coming from the direction of the river harbor. They ran to the Marina Gate just in time to see the giant bird run past. And then the lion. Decimus's father said he thought the lion was a Nubian lion."

Flavia frowned. "A Nubian lion? What does a Nubian lion look like, Nubia? Nubia?"

Jonathan, Lupus, and Flavia looked round the small red kitchen and then out through the ivy-twined columns into the wet green garden.

But Nubia was nowhere to be seen.

"She always does that!" said Jonathan, hitting his forehead with the heel of his hand. "I wish she'd teach me how to disappear like that."

Lupus nodded.

"Nubia!" called Flavia. "NUBIA!"

All they heard was the steady sound of the rain on the terra-cotta roof tiles.

"She's probably just gone upstairs to put on some more tunics," said Flavia. "Let's look for her."

But as they headed for the stairs, Jonathan glanced toward the back door.

"You don't think . . ." he murmured. The others followed his gaze. The back door of Flavia's house was built into the town wall; it led directly into the tombs of the necropolis and the woods beyond. As the three friends moved closer, they could see by a thread of light that it was wedged open.

"Oh no!" cried Flavia.

"She wouldn't be foolish enough to . . ." Jonathan shook his head. "I mean, why would she go into the woods when she knows there might be savage beasts lurking there?"

10

"Aristo!" cried Flavia. "She's gone to warn Aristo!"

Lupus barked, then gestured round the garden and shrugged dramatically, his palms to the sky.

"You're right, Lupus. She's taken the dogs with her."

Jonathan turned to them grimly. "Lupus, you get your sling. I'll get my bow and arrow. We've got to go after her."

"Well, you're not going without me," said Flavia. "Just wait while I get my cloak."

Nubia followed the three dogs into the woods. The rain was lighter under the shelter of the umbrella pines but already there was cold mud squelching between her toes; she was only wearing her house sandals.

"Aristo!" she called. "Aristo, come back!"

She knew he must be somewhere nearby; he had left only a few moments ago. "Aristo! There are wild beasts!"

Her heart was thudding against her ribs and her teeth were chattering. It was not the cold that made her tremble as much as a strange feeling in the pit of her stomach.

Nubia stopped and tried to still the chattering of her teeth so she could listen. Then, as her father had taught her, she reached out with all her senses, not just her sense of hearing.

Presently she had the impression that she should go straight ahead and a little to the left. She knew that this feeling—however vague—was her intuition, so she obeyed it. She moved forward, not calling out now, just listening. The dogs sensed her mood and followed her quietly. Like shadows, they slipped between the rain-glazed trunks of the pine trees. The fine drizzle had stilled all birdsong; the woods were utterly silent.

Then she heard it. A rustling in some myrtle bushes up ahead. Something was moving toward her. Something big.

Cautiously, Nubia moved forward and peered round the wet trunk of an acacia tree. And gasped.

# SCROLL III

Lupus was several paces ahead of his two friends when suddenly Scuto exploded out of the woods.

"Here's Scuto!" said Jonathan.

But Flavia's dog did not stop to greet them. He ran yelping back toward the town walls. Flavia and Jonathan turned and watched him with amazement.

"I've heard the expression 'tail between his legs' before," Flavia said. "But I'd never actually seen it until now. Look! Here come the puppies!"

The two puppies raced past the three friends after Scuto. Then Nubia emerged from the woods, her cloak flapping behind her.

"Run!" she cried. "Big bird is pursuing me!"

Lupus's jaw dropped as a huge black-and-white bird loped out of the woods and stopped to regard him with an enormous long-lashed eye. It had a long white neck and muscular legs. The huge bird clacked its beak and ambled toward him.

"Aaaaah!" Lupus yelled. He turned and ran as fast as he could back toward the safety of the town. He didn't need to urge Flavia and Jonathan to run. They were well ahead of him.

"Man-eating bird!" screamed Flavia, bursting through the back door into her inner garden. "A giant man-eating bird is after us!"

She stood panting and held the door open. Nubia and the dogs were already inside. Lupus charged through a moment later and Jonathan came last, wheezing and gasping. Flavia kicked the wedge out of the way, slammed the door and pressed her back against it.

"Are we all safe?" cried Flavia, breathing hard.

They looked at one another and nodded. The dogs crowded around the gasping friends, snorting and wagging their tails.

"Flavia! What on earth is this commotion!" Her father stepped out of the triclinium and into the garden. The rain had stopped and it was brighter now, although the leaves were still wet and dripping.

"You come in covered in mud, yelling like a fishwife—"

"Pater!" cried Flavia. "Oh Pater! A giant bird . . . a Stymphalian bird! It was the most terrifying thing. . . ." Her voice trailed off as she saw a figure emerge from the study behind him. It was a woman Flavia had never seen before.

Her father turned to the woman.

"Flavia," he said somewhat stiffly. "This is Cartilia Poplicola. Cartilia is a friend of my patron Cordius, and she's recently moved back to Ostia from Rome."

The woman was slender and not very tall, only about Jonathan's height. She had brown eyes and dark hair, pinned up in a simple knot at the back. She wore a cream-colored stola and had wrapped a brown palla round her shoulders. The smile on her face seemed stiff and unnatural.

Flavia disliked her at once.

Her father turned to Cartilia: "That's my daughter Flavia," he sighed. "The one covered in mud."

Flavia looked back at her father. "I can't help it, Pater. I slipped when I was running away from the Stymphalian bird!"

"Don't be silly, Flavia. You know there's no such thing as a Stymphalian bird. If you're trying to embarrass me—"

"No, Pater. It's true. I'm not lying! Am I, Nubia?"

13

"Nubia's just a slave, Flavia," said her father quietly, with a rapid glance at the woman. "I'm sure she'd say whatever you told her to say."

"Pater!"cried Flavia, "I *did* see a Stymphalian bird! And Nubia's not my slave any more. I told you I set her free three months ago when—"

"Flavia!" Her father clenched his jaw. "I want you to take Nubia and go to the baths right now. There's something I need to discuss with you . . ." he glanced at Cartilia again, "and I refuse to talk to you when you're in such a filthy state."

With a sigh of relief, Nubia descended into the circular pool full of hot water.

". . . he might as well have called me a liar," Flavia was saying behind her. "He's never spoken to me like that before."

Nubia nodded and walked to the deepest part. The water in the caldarium of the Baths of Thetis was hot and milky green and smelled of lavender oil. It was wonderful. She sat on the underwater marble shelf and let the steaming water come up to her chin. Then she closed her eyes to let the delicious warmth sink in.

Flavia imitated her father's voice. "I'm sure Nubia would say whatever you told her to!"

Nubia opened her eyes and looked at Flavia, also neck deep in the pool. Flavia's face was quite pink and one or two strands of light brown hair had come unpinned and clung to her neck.

"And he called you a slave! When will he get it through his head that I set you free?"

Nubia closed her eyes again. She knew that when Flavia was upset it was best just to let her talk.

"At least he doesn't treat you like a slave. If he did, I would . . . well, I wouldn't take it!" Flavia paused for a moment and Nubia heard the soothing slap of water against the marble edge of the bath.

"And who was that woman anyway?" muttered Flavia.

Presently, two fat matrons came down the steps into the pool and the water level rose noticeably.

"Come on," grumbled Flavia. "Let's go to the hot rooms."

Nubia pushed through the warm water and carefully followed Flavia up the slippery marble steps. Even though the air in the caldarium was warm, her wet body immediately felt cool. She slipped her feet into the wooden bath clogs. Then, taking up her towel, she hurried into the laconicum after Flavia.

That was better. The laconicum was her favorite room of the baths. It was small and smelled of pine. She liked it when it was so hot and dry she could hardly breathe. It reminded her of the purifying heat of the desert. These past few weeks, sitting in the laconicum or the sudatorium was the only time she felt really warm.

Flavia couldn't take the intense heat of the laconicum, so presently they moved on to the sudatorium. Nubia didn't mind. The sudatorium was hot, too, and steamy. She led Flavia up the tiered marble seats to the one nearest the top: the hottest. She sat and relaxed against the warm marble wall. She wanted to stay here for a long, long time.

"Pater was fine this morning," continued Flavia. "But when we came back—after the bird chased us—it was as if he'd changed. He looked like Pater, but he was acting like someone else! It made me think of how Jupiter disguised himself as Amphitryon. . . ."

Nubia frowned, then nodded as she understood the reference. Hercules.

In lessons yesterday, Aristo had begun to tell them how Jupiter had disguised himself as Hercules' father, Amphitryon, so that he could spend the night with Hercules' mother. Nine months later Hercules had been born. Nubia sighed. Sometimes she found the Greek myths utterly mystifying.

"Maybe," breathed Flavia, ". . . maybe Cartilia is a venefica and has bewitched Pater."

"What is veiny fig?"

"A venefica is a sorceress who uses potions to enchant people: a witch," said Flavia, then added, "I'll bet she's enchanted Pater." There was a long pause and then Flavia said in a small voice. "I wonder what he wants to talk to me about. . . ."

"Flavia," said the sea captain Marcus Flavius Geminus. "Come here."

Flavia went to her father. He stood in the atrium before the household shrine. Flavia had put on her best blue shift and gray leather ankle boots. She wore a dove-gray palla around her shoulders and although her hair was still damp from the baths, she had pinned it up in a simple knot.

For a moment the two of them stood looking at the shrine. It was a wooden cupboard with doors at the front. Inside were the death masks of the Geminus family ancestors. On top of this cupboard were two small marble columns, topped by a wooden pediment and roof, to make it look like a miniature temple.

When she was younger the lararium had seemed huge to her. Now she was as tall as it was. Flavia saw the offerings of the day: a honey cake and a small hyacinth-scented candle. Painted on the wooden back panel of the shrine was a man with a toga draped over his head, the representation of the Geminus family genius. Flavia knew the genius protected the continuity of the family line. The household lares either side of him were shown as windswept young men in fluttering tunics who poured out offerings of wine and grain. Flavia saw the familiar clay statuettes of Castor and Pollux, and of Vesta. At their feet coiled a bronze snake—the protective spirit of the house.

Once, when she was little, her father had found her playing with the sacred images, making up a story in which Castor and Pollux were fighting off the snake who was trying to bite Vesta. Her father had told her they were not toys, but important protectors of the house and family.

Some families worshiped daily at their household shrines. Before his shipwreck, Flavia's father had occasionally lit a candle at the beginning of the day, and made sure the food offering was fresh. But since his return he had become more observant. Now he lit a stick of incense and bowed his head for a moment in prayer.

Presently he turned to her. "Flavia. Do you know the meaning of the word 'piety'?"

"Um, I think so. Aeneas was pious. That meant he was . . . um . . . dutiful."

"Yes, that's right. Being pious means honoring the gods, your family, and the household spirits."

She nodded.

"I know I haven't been the best father to you. I've been away a lot recently. You've had Alma to feed you, Caudex to protect you, and Aristo to educate you . . . but you've obviously felt the absence of a father's discipline. You are very independent and," he glanced down at her, "strong-willed."

Flavia nodded and swallowed.

Her father took the wooden statuette of Castor from the lararium and examined it. "You have disobeyed my orders on several occasions, sometimes endangering your life. And lately you've been running wild. Today was a clear example of that."

Flavia hung her head.

"I love you very much, Flavia. Perhaps too much. I've allowed you to make all sorts of decisions without any reference to me, even though I am the paterfamilias: the head of this family." He sighed. "For example, three months ago you set your new slave girl free on your own initiative—"

"—but Pollius Felix said—"

"—I do not want to hear that name again!" her father shouted, and Flavia recoiled at the vehemence in his voice. "We can't finish one day without you mentioning him. Felix may be a rich and powerful patron, but he is not your father. I am!"

Tears stung Flavia's eyes. Her father hardly ever shouted at her.

He put Castor back and turned to look at her. "Flavia, I am trying to raise you up to be a pious young woman. But you run all over Ostia with a Jew, a beggar boy, and a slave girl, claiming to see giant birds, claiming to solve mysteries, claiming to be some sort of detective! It has to stop."

"What?" Flavia's eyes widened in horror. "What has to stop?"

"I like to think I'm a modern man. I've let you wear a bulla, arranged for you to be educated, entrusted you with a certain measure of independence. But recently I've been criticized for raising you too much like a boy and it seems . . . well, it seems that my critics may have some reason."

"Who?" said Flavia. "Who criticizes you?"

He turned to look down at her. For a terrible moment he seemed like a stranger and Flavia wondered again if someone had bewitched him.

"I'm afraid," said her father, "I'm afraid that from now on I must forbid you to leave the house for any reason, unless you have my express permission."

Flavia opened her mouth, but no sound came out.

"I've also been thinking," said her father, putting his hands on her shoulders, "that it's time we started planning your betrothal. You will soon be of marriageable age and I believe . . ." For the first time during their interview he smiled at her: "I believe I've found a suitable husband for you."

# SCROLL IV

"A husband?" gasped Flavia. "But Pater! I'm only ten years old."

Her father's smile faded. "This would just be a betrothal. I wouldn't expect you to marry him for five or six years yet."

Flavia tried to swallow, but her throat was too dry.

"He's a senator's son," said her father. "Of very good birth. Lives in Rome."

Now Flavia was trembling.

"Apparently he's very studious," continued her father. "He loves books as much as you do. And he's your age."

"My age!" wailed Flavia. "No, Pater! Don't make me marry a baby."

"Flavia! This would be an excellent match for you. Besides, it's your duty to marry. And to have children. It's . . . it's piety!"

"No. I can't." Her heart was banging against her ribs. "I won't marry him!"

Her father sighed. "Then we'll find someone different. Someone older."

"No! I don't want to marry anybody!"

"What?"

"I'm never going to get married!"

"Flavia, you're my last burning coal. If you don't marry and have children you'll be snuffing out your descendants. You'll be snuffing out my descendants." He gestured at the lararium. "You'll be dishonoring our family genius!"

Flavia swallowed hard. "I'm sorry Pater, but I can't," she whispered. "I love someone I can't have, so I'm never, ever getting married."

The look on her father's face was not one of anger. It was one of stunned amazement.

Blinking back tears, Flavia ran out of the atrium and up the stairs to her bedroom.

Jonathan put down the clay doll of a woman he had been examining and picked up one of a gladiator.

He and Lupus were shopping in Ostia's main forum. The market was busy. Ostia's population halved during the months when sailing was impossible. But today it seemed that all the remaining twenty thousand inhabitants were taking advantage of a lull in the rain to buy gifts for the Saturnalia. Men were buying silver, women were buying pickled fruit, slaves and poor people were buying the cheapest gift: candles. And everyone was buying sigilla, the dolls that were the traditional gift of the midwinter festival.

"Hey!" cried Jonathan, and Lupus started guiltily. He'd been lifting the tunic of a girl doll to see what she looked like underneath.

But Jonathan wasn't looking at Lupus. He was examining some sigilla at another stall. "Look at these ones. They're animals. And they're made of wood, not clay."

Lupus put down the sigillum he'd been examining and pushed past a soldier to see.

"Look!" cried Jonathan. "It's the man-eating bird!"

The stall keeper laughed. "That's an ostrich. They don't eat meat. Rumor is one's running around Diana's Grove, outside the Laurentum Gate."

"So *that's* what it was. Hey!" Jonathan turned to Lupus. "We should buy this for Nubia."

Lupus nodded and reached into his coin purse. Jonathan put a hand on his arm.

"Don't use your own money," he said, then lowered his voice. "Father gave me fifty sestercii to buy presents for everyone. For Flavia, Nubia, and Miriam. And you, too, of course. Which one do you like? The wolf? Now what shall we get for Flavia?"

Suddenly Lupus grabbed Jonathan's belt and pulled the older boy after him.

"Watch it!" said a man in a yellow tunic as Lupus shoved past him.

"Sorry, sir," Jonathan said to the man, and to Lupus: "What is it?" Lupus pointed to the sigilla at the next stall. These were also wooden. And painted. Lupus held one up and Jonathan caught his breath. The small jointed doll wore a purple toga and gold wreath. It looked just like the Emperor Titus, whom Jonathan had met two months before.

"Don't touch!" said a voice. "The emperor costs two hundred sestercii. That's real gold leaf on the wreath."

"These are amazing!" said Jonathan, taking the emperor doll from Lupus and carefully replacing it. He looked up at the merchant, a young man in his late teens with hair so fair it was almost white. "Did you paint them?"

"No," said the young man. "A friend of my father's. He sells them up in Rome. He let me bring some to sell here in Ostia. They're images of real people, you know."

Lupus tugged Jonathan's tunic and pointed excitedly to a painted doll of a stout bald man.

"That's admiral Pliny," said the young man. "He died last summer but he used to live around here. He came to our stall in Rome once or twice."

"We knew him," murmured Jonathan, and picked up another figure he recognized: Titus's younger brother Domitian. He felt a jab in the ribs and scowled. "What is it now, Lupus?"

21

Lupus held up one of the dolls.

Jonathan took it wide-eyed, then looked at Lupus.

"I don't believe it," he whispered. "Is it him?"

Lupus grinned and nodded.

"Shall we buy it for Flavia?" he said.

Lupus nodded again.

"How much is this one?" asked Jonathan casually.

"Oh, I don't know who that is. He's only wearing a toga. No gold leaf. Not a senator. Probably a poet. Or somebody's patron. I can let you have it for forty sestercii."

Jonathan nodded and reached for his coin purse. "We'll take— ouch! That was my foot, Lupus!"

Lupus elbowed Jonathan aside and held up both hands.

"Ten?" said the young man to Lupus. "Don't make me laugh. I couldn't sell it for less than thirty."

A quarter of an hour later the boys left the stall with five dolls: a wolf for Lupus, a gladiator for Jonathan, an ostrich for Nubia, a woman with a removable bead necklace for Miriam—and the man in the toga for Flavia.

Lupus had negotiated the lot for fifty sestercii.

"Sorry I can't tell you more about the man in the toga," Pero midus the stall keeper called after them. "I've no idea who he is."

"It doesn't matter." Jonathan grinned at Lupus and added under his breath: "We do."

Nubia was patting Flavia's back when she heard four hollow taps on the bedroom wall.

It was their signal to open the secret passage between their two houses.

Nubia pulled Flavia's bed away from the wall and began to pull out the loose bricks. Bricks were disappearing from the other side, too.

Scuto and Nipur sniffed the growing gap and wagged their tails.

"Hey!" came Jonathan's voice. "Is Flavia crying?"

"Yes," said Nubia. "Her father is telling her to get married. And no more being a detective."

"What?" Jonathan's voice was still muffled. "Why?"

Nubia pulled another brick out. "He says she must be dutiful Roman girl and sit inside. And she mustn't be running all over Ostia with a Jew, a beggar boy, and a slave girl!"

"Poor Flavia!" came Jonathan's voice.

Presently a hand holding a wax tablet appeared. On it Lupus had written:

# I'M NOT A BEGGAR
# I'M A SHIPOWNER!

Finally the breach was big enough for Tigris and the boys to wiggle through. They sat on Flavia's bed, beside Nubia, and the wooden frame creaked alarmingly. Flavia's face was still pressed into the pillow. Outside, it had started to rain again.

"Your father says you can't go out any more?" said Jonathan. "Don't worry, Flavia. You'll think of something. You always do."

Flavia rolled over on her back and looked up at them with red and swollen eyes.

"Want to hear a joke, Flavia?" said Jonathan brightly.

Flavia blinked at him, then nodded.

"How many detectives does it take to light an oil lamp?"

Flavia shook her head.

"Four!" cried Jonathan. "One to solve the mystery of how to light it, and three to . . . um . . . do what she says!"

Nobody laughed, but Flavia sat up.

"Flavia, it's not a very good joke but . . . What I'm trying to say is that we can still solve mysteries. You can be the brains and we'll do the legwork."

"No," sniffed Flavia, wiping her nose on her arm. "You don't understand. I'm a terrible daughter. I've disappointed Pater and now I'll never be a detective again."

"Flavia," said Jonathan. "Lupus and I bought you a present for the Saturnalia, but I think you need it now." He glanced at Lupus who nodded and disappeared back through the hole in the wall. "It might cheer you up," said Jonathan.

Lupus reappeared through the gap. In his hand he held a wooden sigillum of a man wearing a toga.

"Look," said Jonathan with a grin, handing the figure to Flavia.

Flavia took the figure and stared at it in wonder.

Nubia looked too. She saw the blue tunic and white toga, the hair which might have been gray or white-blond, the dots of black paint for the eyes.

Flavia looked up at Jonathan, open-mouthed.

"It's a little doll of the patron. Of Publius Pollius Felix," said Jonathan. "Isn't it good?"

"Oh Jonathan!" Flavia hugged the little doll tightly. "It's wonderful." And she burst into tears.

Flavia must have fallen asleep because the next thing she knew, Nubia was gently shaking her awake.

"Flavia," said Nubia, "Aristo is safely back. He was not eaten by a lion."

"Good," mumbled Flavia, and pulled the blanket up to her chin. The bed was warm and cozy. "What time is it? Have I been asleep?"

"Yes. It is almost time for the betrothal feast. You must get dressed."

Flavia blinked up at her window. She could tell from the light in the room that it was early afternoon.

"Oh!" She groaned and let her head fall back on the pillow. "I can't go. I'm too miserable."

"But Flavia. We have been waiting many weeks for this day. It is the big betrothal day of Miriam."

24

"No," said Flavia, "you go without me." Noble tears welled up in her eyes. She kept her face to the wall and waited for Nubia to persuade her, but there was only silence.

Flavia glanced over her shoulder.

The room was empty.

She sat up, injured. Was that all? Wasn't Nubia going to try harder to convince her? Then Flavia heard her father's feet stomping up the stairs. She quickly lay down again and hugged her new doll so that he wouldn't see it.

"Flavia."

"Yes, Pater," she said in a meek voice.

"Get up and get dressed. This is one of the most important days of your uncle's life and you will not spoil it for him."

"Yes, Pater," said Flavia. She slipped the Felix doll under her pillow and turned to him. "Will you ask Nubia to come up, please?"

"I am here," said Nubia, putting her head into the doorway.

Captain Geminus scowled. "I want you girls downstairs as soon as you're ready. We're late as it is."

"Yes, Pater."

Nubia stepped into the doorway. She was already dressed in a long peach shift worn over a lemon-yellow tunic. Around her hips she had knotted a salmon-pink, red-fringed scarf. And over her shoulders she wore a faded orange palla that had once belonged to Flavia's mother. Nubia wore her tiger's-eye earrings and all her copper bangles. Her short hair had been braided in neat rows running back from her forehead.

"Nubia! You look beautiful! Who did your hair?"

Nubia smiled shyly. "Alma. I am telling her how and she does it very well."

"And you've stained your lips!"

Nubia nodded. "With juice of black currants, like we practiced. Alma helps."

"It should have been me that helped you. And now I don't have time to get ready myself." She picked up the polished silver mirror from her bedside table.

"Oh!" she wailed. "I look terrible! My face is all blotchy and my eyes are red!"

"No," said Nubia loyally. "Red around eyes makes them look more blue."

"Are you girls getting ready?" called a voice from downstairs.

"Yes!" Flavia lied, and pushed the covers back.

Nubia held up Flavia's sky-blue tunic. "I will do your hair but you must put this on quickly."

"Oh, Nubia," said Flavia, as she tried to put some kohl around her puffy eyes, "this has got to be the worst day of my life."

# SCROLL V

Flavia almost forgot her troubles when she stepped into Jonathan's atrium.

She had never seen it so full of people. And she didn't recognize any of them, not even the person who opened the door. The girl was about her age, perhaps a bit younger. She had mousy brown hair and sharp features.

"Shalom," said the girl, and then uttered a stream of words Flavia didn't understand.

Captain Geminus smiled down at the girl. "Sorry," he said. "We don't speak Hebrew." Then he said very slowly. "Do . . . you . . . speak . . . Latin?"

"Of course," said the girl and rolled her eyes. Flavia noticed that one of her eyes was green and the other blue. "I'm Miriam's cousin," said the girl. "My name is Chamat."

"Hello, Chamat," boomed Flavia's father. "I'm Marcus. The groom is my brother. This is my daughter Flavia, her . . . friend Nubia, and her tutor Aristo."

"Captain Geminus!" Jonathan shouldered Chamat aside as he stepped forward. "Shalom." He bowed. "Please come in and enjoy the festivities."

Flavia stared at Jonathan. He was wearing a green silk turban and a cinnamon-colored caftan. His eyes were lightly rimmed with kohl, which made them look very dark and mysterious.

Jonathan stepped back and extended his arm, solemnly inviting his guests to enter. As they filed past him into the atrium he winked at Flavia and Nubia.

Flavia looked around the atrium in wonder. Green garlands had been draped between the white columns around the impluvium. Small round tables were set out with honeyed sesame balls, stuffed dates, and pastries. There were also dice-sized cubes of what looked like marbled flour.

"Halva," said Jonathan, seeing the direction of Flavia's gaze. "Try one."

Flavia did. It was very dense and not too sweet.

"It's made of pressed pistachio and sesame flour," he explained. "My aunt makes the best halva in Italia. She organized the caterers."

Another knock came at the door and Jonathan smiled apologetically. "Excuse me," he said with a little bow to Captain Geminus, then hurried to reach the door before Chamat, who was already undoing the bolt.

Flavia followed her father and Aristo through groups of chatting people. Most of them were dark-haired, with olive skin and black eyes. Although one or two of the men wore turbans and caftans, most were dressed in Roman tunics and capes. They were speaking Latin, Greek, and the language Flavia knew was Hebrew. The women wore stolas or shifts in jeweled colors and some had filmy head scarves.

On the upstairs balcony hired musicians were playing double flute and castanets.

As they passed through a corridor into the columned peristyle that ringed the inner garden, Flavia's eyes opened wide. Two awnings of red canvas had been stretched across either end of the open courtyard, offering additional protection against the fine drizzle that had been falling since noon. These awnings cast a ruby light onto the garden below and made the glossy green shrubs look very dark. Although it was still daytime, oil lamps hung all around the peristyle, burning like stars. As usual, the house smelled of exotic spices: cinnamon, cardamom, mint, and sandalwood.

Aristo stopped abruptly and Flavia bumped into his back.

"Dear Apollo!" she heard him whisper. Flavia peered around him. A crowd of women had parted to reveal Miriam, dressed in her betrothal gown.

Flavia's jaw dropped.

Miriam wore a robe of violet silk embroidered with scarlet and gold thread. Over her head was an embroidered purple scarf hung with dozens of thin gold coins. Miriam's beautiful violet eyes—smoky and kohl-rimmed—smoldered beneath her straight black eyebrows. A tiny sapphire nose stud above her left nostril emphasised the flawless texture of her creamy skin.

"Dear Apollo! She's the most beautiful thing I've ever seen," breathed Aristo.

Miriam smiled when she saw them and stepped forward to greet them.

"Captain Geminus: welcome. And Flavia and Nubia. And Aristo." She lifted her gaze to meet Aristo's and Flavia saw something flicker in Miriam's eyes. Sympathy? Regret?

Miriam was wearing silver bracelets that tinkled as she extended her hand to each of them in turn. As she squeezed Flavia's hand, Flavia saw that her fingers were covered with silver rings.

Flavia suddenly felt shy in the presence of such dazzling beauty. Miriam seemed like a stranger, and far older than her fourteen years.

At that moment Miriam's father approached them.

Doctor Mordecai ben Ezra wore his blue silk caftan and best white turban. He had a sharp nose and a short grizzled beard. His heavy-lidded eyes always reminded Flavia of a turtle's.

"Marcus!" he said in his slightly accented voice. "Welcome! You, too, Aristo. Shalom, Flavia and Nubia. It is good to see you all."

Mordecai gestured toward the study. "Come and have some refreshments." He guided them into the tablinum where they found more groups of chatting guests and more exotic delicacies on trays. There were sesame rings filled with fig paste, candied almonds, and star-shaped aniseed cakes.

Flavia was sucking a honeyed almond and gazing at Miriam when a boy appeared at her elbow with drinks on a tray.

"Thank you," she said, absently taking a cup of hot pomegranate juice.

"Thank you, Lupus," said Nubia beside her, and Flavia turned to stare at the cupbearer.

Lupus was dressed like Jonathan, but his turban was dark blue silk and his caftan pale green. Like Jonathan, he'd lined his eyes with kohl. He gave a mock solemn bow and grinned at them.

"Lupus!" breathed Flavia. "You look so . . . exotic."

The mute boy nodded, wiggled his shoulders, and swayed off exotically into the crowd, still carrying the tray of drinks.

Flavia heard a burst of laughter and her father's voice above the crowd. He sounded cheerful. She turned to see that he'd been joined by his patron Cordius and the woman called Cartilia Poplicola.

Flavia glared at Cartilia. "Who invited her?" she muttered.

At that moment the voices and laughter died away. All eyes turned to the corridor.

Miriam's betrothed had arrived.

Fresh from the baths, Flavia's uncle Gaius wore a pure white toga over his best blue tunic. Tall and tanned, with light brown hair and clear gray eyes, he looked exactly as a Roman should. Even though his nose was broken he was very handsome. Flavia felt a surge of pride, then a pang as her father turned to greet him and the two brothers stood face to face. Although they were identical twins, her father Marcus looked ten years older than his brother. She knew this was partly due to the happiness that lit Gaius's face, but Flavia suddenly saw how much her father had aged in the past few months. He looked like an old man of forty.

Suddenly Flavia's uncle Gaius caught sight of Miriam.

When he saw her his smile faded and his eyes opened wide. The chatter had subsided and the crowd was so quiet that Flavia could hear Miriam jingle as she moved toward Gaius. Miriam stopped shyly before her future husband. They stood for a moment, in the diffused red glow of the awning, gazing into one another's eyes.

"Miriam," began Flavia's uncle, but his voice faltered and he began again. "Miriam daughter of Mordecai, in the presence of all these witnesses, will you be my betrothed?"

Flavia couldn't see Miriam's expression because the embroidered head scarf covered her face. But her low, clear voice said it all.

"Yes, Gaius. In front of all these witnesses I will be your betrothed."

He smiled and took Miriam's extended hand. Solemnly, he slipped a ring onto the fourth finger of her left hand.

Then, still holding her hand in his, Gaius turned so that everyone could see.

Flavia put her mouth close to Nubia's ear, "Once you hold hands in public, it means you are betrothed."

"Kiss her!" cried a woman.

And then a man's voice behind them, "Yes, give her a kiss!"

Miriam lifted her face and as Gaius bent to kiss her, the crowd erupted in rowdy cheers.

Flavia heard a woman behind her tut: "These young people are shameless! In my day a man would not even kiss his wife in public!"

"I know," said the other one. "It's scandalous!" She added with distaste: "And it's obvious they're *in love*."

Flavia glanced behind her to see two dark-haired women. One was short and stout, the other taller, with eyes as green and hard as unripe olives.

They didn't notice her glance and Flavia heard the green-eyed

31

one remark grimly, "It is never a good idea to marry for love."

"Hmmph!" snorted the other woman. "It looks as if the pagan's brother is about to make the same mistake."

Flavia's head jerked around and she stared at her father.

Everyone was crowding around Gaius and Miriam to congratulate them, but her father and Cartilia were oblivious. They stood very close together, smiling and looking into one another's eyes.

And, to her horror, Flavia saw that they were holding hands.

# SCROLL VI

Nubia saw that Flavia's face was as white as chalk.

"I feel sick," said Flavia. "Pater's holding hands with that witch."

Nubia nodded sympathetically.

"No," said Flavia in a strange voice. "I'm really going to be sick. . . ."

Nubia took Flavia's arm and gently pulled her toward the latrine. But the door was shut.

"Nubia!" Flavia covered her mouth with her hand.

Thinking quickly, Nubia pulled Flavia through Jonathan's back door. Someone had wedged it partially open. They were just in time.

Flavia bent over and vomited onto the wet grasses. Nubia gently held her friend's head and whispered soothing words in her own language. When Flavia had finished, she began to shiver, so Nubia put her arms around her.

"Pater was holding her hand," Flavia said to Nubia in a small voice. "That means he's going to ask her to marry him . . . if he hasn't already."

Nubia nodded. "Be happy for him," she said.

"How can I be happy," whispered Flavia. "I don't even know who she is."

"Come," said Nubia. "I am taking you home."

It was only as she turned to guide Flavia back into the house that Nubia saw Aristo further along the wall. He was leaning against the rough, damp bricks of the town wall.

Aristo's eyes were closed and his face lifted to the sky. Like Flavia, he had wet cheeks, but Nubia could not tell whether from rain or from tears.

The sounds of revelry and music from next door kept Flavia awake well into the night. Presently her tears dried and she began to think. She rolled onto her back and stared up at the slanting timbers of her roof, dim in the light of a single oil lamp.

Someone had been criticizing her father for giving her too much freedom. And as far as she knew there was only one new person in his life: Cartilia.

It must be Cartilia's fault that she was now to be kept like a prisoner in her own home. It was Cartilia who had put an end to her detective work. Cartilia who wanted her to be a dutiful Roman daughter.

Suddenly Flavia had a thought that made her gasp. Her father wanted her to marry a senator's son from Rome. How did he know a senator? He hardly ever went up to Rome. But Cartilia had been living in Rome. The marriage was probably her idea to get Flavia out of the way.

"That witch wants Pater all to herself," Flavia murmured.

At the foot of her bed Scuto raised his head and looked at her.

"But why?" whispered Flavia.

Scuto thumped his tail.

"I've got to find out." Flavia rolled over on her side and looked at her Felix doll. "If I can prove to Pater that she's evil, then maybe he'll let me keep solving mysteries. And maybe he won't make me marry someone else. Then things can stay just the way they are."

The doll's dark eyes seemed to gaze back at her.

"This is a mystery," she told the doll, "and I've got to solve it. If Pater won't allow me to go out without his permission, then I'll just have to get it."

"Is it safe to come in?" whispered Jonathan, pushing his head through the wall.

Flavia nodded. "Pater and Uncle Gaius and Caudex have gone to Laurentum to finish getting the Lodge ready."

Jonathan crawled through the breech in the wall, greeted Scuto and Nipur, and helped Lupus come through. "We've been helping Father clean up after the party," he explained as he flopped onto Flavia's bed. "And he said we could take a break." He sighed. "Sometimes I wish we had slaves like everybody else."

Lupus nodded his agreement and sat beside Nubia on her bed. She was wearing five tunics and had a blanket wrapped around her shoulders. It was noon: damp, gray, and cold.

"Isn't Miriam helping you?" asked Flavia. "After all, it was her party."

"No," said Jonathan mildly, "Miriam's gone to stay with my two aunts. They're going to help her get ready for the wedding."

"Is one of them a woman with eyes like olives?" asked Flavia, pulling her blue palla tighter around her shoulders.

Jonathan nodded. "That's Keturah. Father's eldest sister. He's a bit frightened of her."

"I don't blame him," muttered Flavia. "Anyway," she added, "Nubia and I will help you clean up. Pater said we could go to your house today. That's the only place we're allowed to go. Plus the baths." She rested her chin in her hands and stared glumly at the wall. "At least he's not spending the day with *Cartilia*." She sneered as she pronounced the name.

"Who is Cartilia, anyway?" asked Jonathan.

"She's the one who's convinced Pater I'm running wild. It's her fault I'm trapped in this house like a bird in a cage."

35

"How do you know it's her fault?" asked Jonathan.

"It's obvious. Pater tells me someone's been criticizing him for the way he's raising me and a few hours later he introduces me to that woman. I'm sure it's her idea to marry me off, as well."

"Who are you supposed to marry?" Jonathan scratched Scuto behind the ear.

Flavia snorted. "Some boy my age who lives in Rome. Apparently we'll get on because we both like reading." Flavia hugged her knees and grumbled: "She probably doesn't even love him. She's probably after the money we don't have."

"Who?"

"Cartilia, of course. If only I could do some investigating. I'm sure I could expose Cartilia for what she really is."

Lupus uttered a bark of laughter.

Flavia looked at him. "What?"

He scribbled on his wax tablet and held it up:

## SATURNALIA!!

"Everybody is talking Saturnalia," said Nubia. "But I am still not knowing who she is."

Jonathan grinned. "The Saturnalia," he said, "is the Roman festival where everybody worships the god Saturn and asks him to make the days longer again."

Flavia nodded. "People give each other gifts and gambling is allowed and we don't have lessons—"

"I like lessons," said Nubia.

"—and," continued Flavia, "slaves trade places with their masters and everything is upside down and back to front."

Lupus had been writing throughout this exchange:

## DON'T YOU CHOOSE KING OF THE SATURNALIA TONIGHT?

"Lupus," cried Flavia. "You're brilliant!"

"What?" asked Nubia.

Flavia turned to her. "On the night before the Saturnalia each household chooses a king of the Saturnalia. It can be anybody from the lowest slave to the master. Then, for the five days of the Saturnalia everyone *has to do what the king says!*"

Lupus was nodding vigorously.

"If I were chosen," said Flavia. "I could do as I liked! Within reason. . . ." Then her face fell. "But I might not be chosen."

"A girl can be king?" asked Nubia, her amber eyes wide.

"Yes," said Flavia. "Anybody can be chosen. Then they're king for the remaining five days of the festival."

"Sounds crazy to me," said Jonathan.

Flavia nodded. "Once, when Nero was emperor, he fixed it so that he was elected king of the Saturnalia. Then he made everyone do the things they hated most, like singing in public or eating their worst food. . . ."

"He was already emperor and he had to be king of the Saturnalia, too?" Jonathan raised his eyebrows. "What a big bully."

"How are they choosing the king of the Saturnalia?" asked Nubia.

"By a throw of the dice," said Flavia.

"So how did Nero get himself chosen?" asked Jonathan.

"Oh, he cheated," said Flavia. "He found a loaded die, and . . ." Her eyes opened wide. "If only we had a loaded die," she breathed.

"What is low dead die?" asked Nubia, with a look of concern.

## NOT LOADED, SHAVED

wrote Lupus. Then, with a mischievous grin, he reached into the pouch at his belt and held up a small ivory cube with black dots painted on each face.

Flavia's eyes grew wide as he blew on it and tossed it onto the bedroom floor. Then she squealed and gave Lupus a hug.

The die had come up six.

# SCROLL VII

"Sex!" cried Flavia Gemina.

"Tres!" said her father with a smile, relieved to see his daughter in good spirits again.

"Quattuor," mumbled Caudex, standing in the wide doorway of the dining room.

"Quinque," said Alma and nodded at the others. "It's my lucky number."

"Duo," said Nubia, and looked expectantly at Aristo.

"Your turn, Aristo," said Flavia.

"What?" He frowned absently and looked at them.

"We're throwing the die to choose the king of the Saturnalia," said Flavia patiently. "Choose a number."

Aristo adjusted his ivy garland. "Sex."

"I've already chosen that number. The only number left is unus."

"Then I must be unus." He sighed.

"Now where did I put those dice?" muttered Captain Geminus. "They were here a moment ago. . . ."

Lupus tried to look innocent.

"Great Neptune's beard! I put them right on this table. Have you seen them, Caudex?"

"No, master." Caudex looked confused.

Lupus fished in his belt pouch, held up his die, and raised his eyebrows at Flavia's father.

"Thank goodness someone has their wits about them," said Captain Geminus. "Lupus, would you do us the honor of throwing the die?"

Lupus nodded, blew on the die, and threw it onto the marble-topped table. It came up six.

"*Euge!*" squealed Flavia. "I'm the king of the Saturnalia!"

"Congratulations, Flavia!" cried Jonathan, and Lupus clapped loudly.

Flavia's father gave her a long look, then sighed deeply. "I don't know how you did it, Flavia. But you managed to buy yourself five more days of freedom. I suggest you act wisely. I am still your father and the head of this household."

"Don't worry, Pater," said Flavia, lifting her chin. "I won't be a tyrant. I promise I'll use my powers for good."

Lupus was glad to be wearing his new fur-lined boots. The first day of the Saturnalia had dawned clear and bright, but very cold.

Although Jonathan's family didn't observe the other traditions of the Saturnalia, Mordecai had given each of Jonathan's three friends a seasonal gift of soft leather boots lined with fox fur.

The four friends stood on Flavia's front porch. They wore their warmest clothes. Nubia had on all the tunics she owned, plus a pair of Captain Geminus's woolen leggings which had shrunk at the fuller's. She also had one of the captain's old woolen cloaks wrapped around her.

"Before we start investigating Cartilia," said Flavia, "we're going to watch the ceremony at the Temple of Saturn. Pater gave me permission to go."

Flavia stepped off the porch and started along the cold pavement toward the fountain. Lupus and the others fell into step beside her. Up and down the street, other people were emerging from their houses, their breath coming in white puffs as they called out the traditional greeting: "Yo, Saturnalia!"

"Pater told me that Cartilia is a widow," said Flavia. "She grew up here in Ostia but then she married a lawyer and they moved to Rome. Pater said her husband died a few years ago and they never had any children, so she moved back here."

Three men wearing colorful cloaks and soft conical hats were staggering toward them, going against the flow. "Yo, Saturnalia!" they cried happily and Lupus could smell the wine on their breath.

"Yo, Saturnalia!" replied Flavia and Nubia.

"They've started celebrating early!" muttered Jonathan.

"Pater told me Cartilia is staying with her parents here in Ostia," continued Flavia. "But when I asked him where they lived he gave me one of his looks. I think he was beginning to get suspicious. That's the first thing we need to find out: where Cartilia's parents' house is."

"Did you ask Alma?" said Jonathan.

"She doesn't know anything." Flavia frowned. "Or she's not telling. Even though I made her breakfast today."

"I helped," said Nubia. "We made the poculum."

"Pater's gone to Laurentum again, but before he left I suggested he invite Cartilia to dinner this afternoon. He seemed pleased about that, and when I asked if we could go and watch the sacrifice this morning he said yes. He said we didn't even have to take a body-guard. Since Venalicius died there hasn't been a single kidnapping!"

As they turned into Bakers Street, two pretty young women danced out of a tavern.

"Yo, Saturnalia!" they giggled. One of them darted forward to kiss Jonathan on the cheek.

"Yo!" He jumped back surprised, and then blushed as she smiled at him.

The other woman patted Lupus's head. "Sweet little boy!"

Lupus snarled at her and the two of them ran giggling toward Ostia's main street.

"I've decided I like the Saturnalia," remarked Jonathan. Lupus scowled.

"Great Neptune's beard!" exclaimed Flavia.

They had come out onto the Decumanus Maximus. It was full of people, all making their way toward the temple. The people of Ostia—both slaves and free—were dressed in their best winter clothes: long tunics, soft leather shoes, and thick woolen cloaks. Many of them wore the conical felt hats that slaves wore after they had been set free. The hats were red, blue, green, and yellow.

"Yo, Saturnalia!" came the cry on all sides.

As the friends approached the theater, Lupus heard the sound of drums, flutes, and bells. Soon they caught up with a troupe of musicians playing a discordant tune with a strong beat. There were four men and a woman, all dressed in green tunics with matching leather boots. The woman wore an anklet of bells that jingled rhythmically as she danced. Lupus stopped to watch her for a moment before the crowd swept the four friends along with it.

Presently they found themselves in a sacred precinct just past the theater. Before them were four small temples.

Lupus snarled again as a man stepped on his new boot. Lupus hated crowds. Looking around, he caught sight of a covered fountain built against a wall. In a moment he had clambered up onto its vaulted roof.

That was better. Now he had a perfect view of the little Temple of Saturn with its black marble columns and the cult statue.

"Hey, Lupus!" cried Jonathan. "Give me a hand up."

A moment later the four friends all sat on the fountain's roof, looking over the heads of the crowd as the priest of Saturn appeared beside the cult statue.

The priest was intoning something. Lupus caught a phrase above the excited babble of the crowd: ". . . today when the old order is restored so that the sun may return and the days grow longer. . . ." Most people ignored the priest to catch up on gossip. But the happy buzz of the crowd grew quieter as the priest's assistants brought a dozen sacred piglets forward. This was of interest to them: After the piglets had been sacrificed their flesh would be roasted for a public feast.

Lupus knew that sacrificial animals were usually drugged to make them sleepy, but the small pink creatures seemed unusually nervous. As the piglets were carried up the steps, Lupus caught a glimpse of their rolling eyes and twitching noses. Suddenly one of them uttered a high-pitched squeal and writhed free.

There were screams of laughter as the rogue piglet charged the crowd.

"Come back, you!" shouted the attendant. "We want to read your entrails!" He plunged into the crowd after the piglet. Lupus could see the crowd parting before the fugitive.

"Dignity!" bellowed the priest of Saturn from the top of the temple steps. "Dignity and decorum. Nothing must spoil the sanctity of the sacrifice!"

Ignoring him, two other piglets also squirmed out of the arms locked around them.

One disappeared down a side street and the other set off back toward the theater, his little trotters twinkling as he ran.

"He's off to Rome!" quipped a woman.

"You're too late for the races!" a man called after the piglet.

The crowd laughed.

Then a woman screamed. Below Lupus a man uttered an oath and pointed toward the temple steps. A tawny beast had appeared from behind a black column.

"Lion!" came a woman's hysterical voice. "It's the escaped lion!"

# SCROLL VIII

"Lion!" screamed a voice in the crowd. "Run for your lives."

As the people below them started to run, Nubia turned to her friends.

"Don't go down!" she cried. "We will be squashed!"

Lupus was halfway off the fountain, about to drop to the ground. He stared wildly up at Nubia, then nodded. They helped him back up.

Within moments the square before the temple was deserted, apart from half a dozen people who'd been trampled in the stampede. One of them was a little boy, no more than four years old. He lay on the cold paving stones, whimpering for his mother.

Nubia kept her eyes on the lion. He was padding slowly down the temple steps. The priest had disappeared. His attendants, too.

"Look at his stomach," Nubia said to the others. "He is very fulled."

"She's right," gulped Jonathan. "Either that or she's pregnant!"

"Not she," said Nubia. "He. Behold the . . . hair?" Nubia didn't know the Latin word.

"The mane?" Flavia was trembling. "That means it's a boy lion?"
Nubia nodded.

"Can lions jump up?" asked Jonathan nervously.

Nubia shook her head. "Lions are not so good climbers."

The lion had reached the bottom step of the temple. Even from across the square Nubia could smell his strong musky scent. He lifted his nose and tested the air, just as her puppy Nipur sometimes did.

The boy's crying was louder now. The lion turned his head, then began to move toward the child.

Nubia's heart was pounding. She knew she had to act now. The lion had obviously eaten recently, so he probably was not hungry. But a wounded creature was always of interest to a meat-eater. She hoped her father's advice for stopping a lion was correct.

Nubia slipped off the fountain and landed lightly on her feet. The lion stopped and slowly turned his big head. For a moment his golden eyes locked with Nubia's, but they betrayed no flicker of interest in her. He turned his head again and padded slowly toward the little boy.

"Nubia!" hissed Flavia. "What are you doing?"

Slowly and without taking her eyes from the lion, Nubia unwrapped the nutmeg-colored cloak from her shoulders. Then she walked cautiously toward the boy on the ground. He had stopped crying but was shaking in terror. The lion glanced at her but did not stop moving forward.

Nubia and the lion converged, and when she and the lion were no more than two yards from the shivering child, Nubia tossed her cloak. The lion froze as the cloak fell over his head and shoulders. For a moment he remained motionless. Then he slowly lifted one great paw and tried to pull off the cloak.

"Get him, boys! Now!" The voice came from behind Nubia, along with the sound of running footsteps and the grating of wheels on paving stones. She turned to see a squad of six soldiers run forward. They were pulling a large wooden box on wheels. A brown-skinned man with a whip ran after them.

"Stop there, boys!" he cried. "Wait for my order!"

The soldiers stopped and the man—he looked Syrian—cracked his whip. "Stay, Monobaz!" he cried. "Stay!"

The lion stopped trying to paw the cloak from its head and waited obediently.

"Put the cage right in front of him," commanded the Syrian, "and raise the door."

The soldiers obeyed. Then one of them fainted.

"Good boy," murmured the Syrian, while the soldiers attended to their fallen comrade.

The tamer moved toward the lion. "Good Monobaz."

Slowly he pulled Nubia's cloak from the lion's massive head. "Good boy. Into your cage, Monobaz. Nice piece of calf's liver in there for you."

The lion looked up at him with yellow eyes, blinked, and disappeared into the box. Now only his tail was visible, writhing and twitching like a tawny snake. The tamer pushed the lion's curling tail in and slid the door shut. Then he turned to Nubia and held out her cloak.

"My dear girl," he said, "I don't know who you are or where you come from, but you deserve a golden victor's wreath. That was the wisest thing you could have done. And the bravest!"

Flavia hugged Nubia. "You're a hero," she said. "You saved us all!"

The little boy's hysterical mother had carried her child away without even thanking Nubia, but the lion tamer stayed to express his gratitude.

"You saved my skin," he said. "My name's Mnason. I'm Monobaz's owner."

Flavia looked him up and down. He had light brown skin, dark hair slick with oil, and a neat pointed beard.

"I'm Flavia Gemina," she said, "daughter of Marcus Flavius Geminus, sea captain. This is Jonathan, Lupus, and Nubia the heroine."

"Delighted to meet you all. Especially you, Nubia. May I ask how you knew to throw a cloak over his head?"

"My father told me," said Nubia solemnly.

"I'd like to congratulate him on the bravery of his daughter!"

Nubia dropped her head and Flavia whispered, "You can't. Her father's dead."

"Oh, I'm sorry," said Mnason. He tugged his ear and Flavia noticed he wore three gold earrings in it.

The people were beginning to return. Vigiles were putting the injured people on stretchers, and the head priest had poked his head cautiously around the side of the temple.

"Listen," said Mnason to Nubia. "I'd like to reward you. But I see the magistrate is coming my way. Can you meet me at noon in the Forum of the Corporations? At the corporation of beast importers?"

Nubia looked at Flavia.

"Of course!" said Flavia.

"Good. Now, before he gets here, tell me. You four haven't seen a camelopard anywhere around here, have you?"

Lupus knew that the Forum of Corporations was behind the theater near the river. He led his friends through the arched entrance. A porter appeared and Flavia stepped forward.

"We've come to see Mnason," she said politely. "He's expecting us."

"At the Corpse of the Beast Importers," added Nubia.

"Hey! You're the brave girl who caught the lion! Everyone's talking about it!" said the porter. "Mnason and his lion are just over there. Near the temple."

He gestured toward a pretty temple in the middle of a grassy rectangle. Lupus knew it was the Temple of Ceres, the goddess of grain. Grain was Ostia's lifeblood, and the main reason for the town's existence. Without a port to receive the grain ships from Egypt, docks to unload it, and warehouses to store it, Rome's million inhabitants would go without bread.

Around the grassy precinct of the temple was a three-story

colonnade that housed Ostia's various corporations. Flavia's father had once told Lupus that "corporation" meant a group of people. There were the shipbuilders and owners; the tanners, rope makers and sailors; the measurers and importers of grain; and the importers of other useful products: olive oil, wine, honey, marble, and exotic beasts.

Lupus liked the Forum of the Corporations because of the black-and-white mosaics beneath the covered colonnade at ground level. He often copied the pictures of animals, ships, and buildings onto his wax tablet. There were mosaics of tigers, lions, hunting dogs, and his favorite, the elephant. To his delight, he saw that was where Mnason sat: at the corporation of beast importers. The tamer sat just outside the colonnade on a folding leather chair, his eyes half closed in the thin winter sunshine. He had a cup of steaming wine in one hand and a wax tablet in the other. Monobaz the lion paced up and down in his wooden cage nearby.

When Mnason saw them approaching his dark eyes widened and he leaped out of his chair.

"Welcome, young friends," he greeted them. "A cup of hot wine? It is the Saturnalia, after all!"

Flavia shook her head. "I need a clear head," she said. "But thank you."

Lupus stepped closer to the lion's cage and the others followed.

"Nubia," said the lion tamer. "Thank you again for your bravery. Monobaz is gentle as a lamb, but people don't know that. Someone might have killed him. How can I reward you?"

Nubia looked at him shyly. "May I stroke him?"

"Of course. Is that all you want?"

Nubia nodded and shivered.

"You're not afraid of him, are you?" asked Mnason.

"No," whispered Nubia. "I am just cold."

"Come here, Monobaz. Look! Just scratch him behind the ear. He's like a big kitten."

47

"Oh," giggled Nubia. "He is making a big purring."

Mnason grinned. "I told you. Lions are just big cats."

"Except cats don't bite your arm off at the elbow," said Jonathan.

"May I ask a question?" said Flavia.

"Anything for a friend of Nubia's," said Mnason.

"Do you know of a woman named Cartilia Poplicola?" asked Flavia.

"That's an unusual question!" said Mnason. "Most people ask me if Monobaz is a man-eater!"

"It's for an investigation. I'm—" Flavia's eyes widened: "Is Monobaz a man-eater?"

Mnason laughed. "Of course not."

Jonathan turned to look at the trainer. "Then what's in his stomach?"

"A sheep," said Mnason, his expression becoming serious. "They found its remains yesterday. I'll have to compensate the owner. But Monobaz would never eat a person. He's as tame as a big kitten. In fact, I'm teaching him to hold a live rabbit in his mouth." He saw Flavia looking at him and raised his eyebrows.

"Cartilia," she said patiently. "Cartilia Poplicola?"

"I'm not a native of Ostia," he said, "but everyone knows the Poplicola family. They've been here for generations. The harbor master is called Lucius Cartilius Poplicola."

"I know," said Flavia. "But he's not married."

"Well," said Mnason, "his brother Quintus is a chief grain measurer. He might be Cartilia's father, or husband, if she took his name. . . ."

"Her husband's dead," said Flavia.

"Then it must be her father," said Mnason. "I don't know much about him. But I do believe his corporation is that one there, right across the square. You'll recognize it by the mosaic of a man measuring grain."

"Thank you, sir," said Flavia and started across the grass. Lupus

48

tapped her on the shoulder and showed her his wax tablet. Flavia read the question he had written there and turned back to the Syrian. "Just one more question," she said politely.

"Yes?"

"What does a camelopard look like?"

"Cartilia Poplicola?" The dark-skinned African frowned and scratched his head. Behind him and the column he leaned against, a group of men were drinking and laughing. Flavia could hear the rattle of dice and the clink of coins. She knew the Saturnalia was the only time when gambling was legally permitted.

Flavia studied the African. He had a bald head with two alarming bumps in it: one over his left ear and one over his right eye. "Which Cartilia Poplicola?" he said.

"There are more than one?" Flavia tried not to stare at the lump on his forehead; it was the size of a chestnut.

"My master has three daughters. All called Cartilia Poplicola. Is she the youngest?"

"Maybe."

Bumpy-head glanced around, then leaned forward. "He's always moaning about one of them." Flavia could smell the wine on his breath. "He says she's a bit demented."

"Demented like insane?"

He shrugged, then nodded.

"Which one is that?" asked Flavia.

"I'm not positive, but I think her nickname is Paula."

# SCROLL IX

"Nubia! Look out!" screamed Flavia Gemina. She pressed a hand to her heart. "You almost dropped some eggshell in the bowl."

"No," said Nubia patiently. "There is no eggshell." She sighed. She wasn't enjoying herself. They were supposed to be making omelettes for the first course of the feast. Flavia might be a good detective, but she was not a very good cook.

Nubia shivered. Even though she had all her tunics on, she was still cold. And damp. Nothing ever seemed to get really dry. The only good thing about preparing dinner was that she could stand near the glowing coals of the kitchen hearth.

Alma was in the garden, loitering near the quince bush, pretending to look for any remaining fruit. Nubia knew she missed being in her kitchen.

"It's all right, Alma," said Flavia, without looking up. "I'm not going to break anything. Oh look! Saffron. Can we use some in the stew?"

"Be careful, dear." Alma abandoned the quince bush and hurried to the doorway of the kitchen. Nubia glanced up from beating the eggs in time to see the look of dismay on Alma's face as Flavia dropped six thin red filaments of saffron in the stew.

"Saffron is terribly expensive. . . ." Alma's voice trailed off.

"Don't worry!" said Flavia brightly. "You only have a Saturnalia feast once a year . . . er, well, five afternoons a year."

50

"You're going to cook again tomorrow?" said Alma in a small voice.

"Of course! We'll cook every day this week. We want you and Caudex to have a nice rest. Don't we, Nubia? Nubia!" Flavia turned away from her stew and wrenched the ceramic bowl from Nubia's hands. "Don't beat the eggs like *that*. Beat them like *this*."

The dogs sped joyfully across the cold ground, barking as they went.

Nubia breathed a sigh of relief. Dogs were so simple and uncomplicated. They never told you what to do. They just loved you.

She was glad she could go into the woods again. Monobaz the lion was safely in his cage, everyone said the ostrich was not dangerous, and the camelopard had not been sighted since it loped off down the beach.

Nubia looked up at the sky. It was a sky unlike any she had ever seen before: very low, with swollen layers of bruised pink clouds all moving at different speeds. It was not long after noon, but already the light was fading. And it was cold. Always cold. She pulled her cloak tighter around her shoulders.

As Nubia followed the dogs into the woods, she inhaled. She loved the spicy fresh scent of the umbrella pines, and she knew she would always associate that smell with Ostia.

"Ostia." She whispered the name to herself. It was a bittersweet word. It was her new home and she loved it, but sometimes she missed the clean hot sands of the desert and its infinite sky full of burning stars.

Suddenly Nubia stopped.

She had heard the snap of a twig. And a low moan.

It was not the dogs; they were off to her left, urgently sniffing the base of an acacia tree.

Was it the ostrich again? The camelopard?

Nubia heard the distant moan again.

Silently she stepped forward, then put out a hand to steady herself against an umbrella pine.

51

The couple were quite a distance away. A man and a woman, locked in a passionate embrace. Nubia felt the hot rush of blood to her face. She moved closer to the tree. The rough, wet bark of its trunk was cool against her cheek. She couldn't see the face of the woman in the dark hooded cloak, but when the man moved a little she saw his curly hair and short red hunting cape.

It was Aristo.

"So, Cartilia," said Flavia Gemina, setting a platter of omelettes on the table in front of the central couch. "Tell us about yourself. Tell us everything." Flavia and Nubia had prepared the first feast of the Saturnalia all by themselves. Nubia was in the kitchen garnishing the main course while Flavia served the starter.

As she stepped back, Flavia saw her father frown. He was reclining next to Cartilia. Aristo occupied the right-hand couch and Alma and Caudex reclined rather stiffly on the left-hand couch.

Jonathan and Lupus were not with them; they were at home, observing the start of the Sabbath with Mordecai.

"Do you have a big family?" Flavia asked Cartilia sweetly, ignoring her father's warning look.

Cartilia swallowed a bite of omelette. "Yes. There are five of us. My father and mother, me, and my two sisters. My poor father is surrounded by women."

Flavia laughed heartily, then stopped. "And what does your father do?" she asked.

"He's one of Ostia's main agents for the grain business." Cartilia took another bite of her omelette. Flavia glanced around at the others.

"Hey!" she said. "Why aren't the rest of you eating your omelettes?"

"It's a little too salty for me," said Aristo. He put down his spoon.

"And terribly fishy, Flavia," said her father.

"And a bit slimy," mumbled Caudex. "Don't like slimy egg. Makes my throat close up."

Alma sighed and pressed her lips together.

"Well," said Flavia defensively, "the recipe called for lots of garum. And I had a little accident with the salt pot. Watch out for shards of clay."

Flavia turned back to Cartilia and nodded with approval as the woman dug in.

"So," she prompted. "You have two sisters."

"Yes," said Cartilia. "I'm the eldest. My middle sister is married. She lives in Bononia, up in the north. And my younger sister Diana lives here in Ostia. She's not married yet, even though she's almost eighteen. She still lives with my parents."

Nubia came into the room with the next course, lentil and chicken stew.

"Where do your parents live? Do you live there too?" asked Flavia.

Cartilia nodded. "We own one of the old houses behind the Temple of Rome and Augustus."

Suddenly Flavia frowned. "Your sister's name is Diana? I thought you were all called Cartilia."

"We are," said Cartilia with a smile, mopping up the last of her runny omelette with a piece of charred bread. "Diana is just her nickname."

"And do you have a nickname?"

"Yes," said Cartilia brightly. "My parents call me Paula."

With a sharp intake of breath, Flavia glanced over at Nubia, who was serving the stew.

"And what was your husband's name again?" she asked.

Cartilia's smile faded. "Postumus," she said quietly. "Postumus Sergius Caldus."

"Was his death sudden?"

"Flavia!"

"Sorry, Pater," said Flavia.

But she had seen the blood drain from Cartilia's cheeks and she was not sorry at all.

■■■

"There's something fishy about her and it's not from my omelette," whispered Flavia to her Felix doll. "She smiles too much."

It was dark and Nubia's breathing came steadily from the bed nearby. The dogs were asleep, too, curled up at the foot of the beds. But Flavia's mind was still too active for her to sleep.

"And she seemed very nervous when I mentioned her dead husband."

In the flickering light of a close-trimmed oil lamp, the doll's eyes seemed to gaze back at her. "If I can prove to Pater that she's not what she seems, then maybe he'll let me keep solving mysteries. And maybe he won't make me marry someone else. Then things can stay just the way they are."

Flavia snuggled down under her woolen blanket and looked at the doll's little face for a moment. It really was a remarkable likeness. "Goodnight, Felix," she whispered. "I hope I dream about you tonight."

That night Flavia did dream. But it was not about Felix.

It was her old nightmare. Dogs were pursuing her through the woods on a steep mountainside. She ran and ran. At last she emerged into a clearing and skidded to a halt at the cliff edge. Below her the sea crashed onto jagged rocks. No escape that way.

She turned just in time to see a black-maned lion explode from the woods and launch himself at her. As Flavia tried to scream, a muscular man in a loincloth tackled the lion and wrestled it to the ground. Helplessly, Flavia watched them struggle, gripping one another with straining muscles and bared teeth. At last the lion lay limp on the ground, and the hero turned to face her. He had gray-blue eyes and hair the same color as the lion's tawny pelt. His bulging muscles gleamed with sweat and his brave chest rose and fell as he caught his breath. She knew it was Hercules.

"Flavia Gemina," he said. "With my help, you have accomplished the first task. But you must complete eleven more, just as I did."

54

"What?"

"You must complete twelve tasks. Thus will you atone for your offense."

"What offense?" cried Flavia in her dream. "What have I done wrong?"

Hercules looked at her and shook his head sadly. "Your crime and mine are the same," he said.

And then he flew away.

# SCROLL X

"And then he flew away?" said Jonathan.

Flavia nodded solemnly. It was the second day of the Saturnalia and the four friends were sitting on a dining couch in her triclinium watching the wall painter work. He had whitewashed the first wall the day before and now he was making sketches with a twig of willow charcoal.

Jonathan frowned: "And you think the dream was sent by the gods?"

"Definitely."

"And in your dream Hercules said you had to atone for some offense? Like a sin?"

Flavia nodded again and Jonathan noticed she held the Felix doll in her lap.

## WHAT OFFENSE?

Lupus scrawled on his wax tablet.

"I've been thinking about it," said Flavia. "I think my crime is the same one that Hercules committed."

"But Aristo is telling us that Hercules killed his family," said Nubia.

"And you obviously haven't killed your family," chuckled Jonathan. His smile faded as Flavia nodded.

"That's exactly what I've done."

Her three friends looked at her wide-eyed.

"I told Pater I would never marry and he said that I was killing my descendants. Don't you see?" She looked around at her friends' puzzled faces. "I'm Pater's last burning coal and if I don't marry then I've killed my future family!"

"You're never getting married?" said Jonathan. "Not ever?"

Flavia looked down at the Felix doll. "No," she whispered. "I love someone I can never have."

"So Hercules came to you in a dream and said you have to complete twelve tasks. What tasks?"

Flavia lowered her voice. "I think I know what I have to do. That woman Cartilia has bewitched Pater. She wants to marry him and get me out of the way. I need to find out why and I need to stop her. Then everything will be the way it was and Pater will be happy again. I think the twelve tasks will provide the clues I need to stop her."

"What are the tasks Hercules had to do?" asked Nubia.

"His first task was to kill a huge lion with his bare hands. I haven't killed a lion, but you overpowered one, Nubia, and that led us to some clues: Cartilia's nickname is Paula and she's a bit demented. Now let me see if I can remember the other tasks. Aristo was teaching us a special way to remember them in order . . ."

Lupus raised his hand and eagerly began writing on his wax tablet.

# LION
# HYDRA
# DEER
# BOAR
# STABLES
# MAN-EATING BIRDS

"That's right!" said Flavia. "Hercules' second task was to kill a monster called the hydra, his third was to capture a deer sacred to Diana, his fourth was to capture a fierce boar, his fifth was to clean the stables, and his sixth was to kill the man-eating Stymphalian birds." Flavia paused and frowned.

"Impressive!" said Jonathan, looking at Lupus's wax tablet. "Are you using Aristo's method?"

Lupus nodded and gave them a smug grin. He had completed the list.

## CRETAN BULL
## MAN-EATING HORSES
## AMAZON'S BELT
## RED CATTLE
## GOLDEN APPLES
## CERBERUS

Flavia nodded. "That's right, Lupus! Task seven was to capture the Cretan bull, task eight to capture some man-eating horses, task nine to get the Amazon's belt, ten was to capture the red cattle—they were sacred to Juno. His last two tasks were to get the golden apples of the Hesperides at the end of the world and to bring Cerberus the three-headed dog up from Hades."

Jonathan frowned. "So does that mean you have to kill a hydra and capture a deer and go to the ends of the world to fetch some apples?"

"I don't think I have to actually DO the tasks," said Flavia. "Hercules has done them already. But each task will give me a clue to help me find the truth about Cartilia."

"It sounds a bit crazy to me."

"Maybe," said Flavia, "but when I came downstairs this morning the gods gave me another sign as a confirmation." She pointed to the wall painter. "Him. Hercules the wall painter."

"He's called Hercules?" Jonathan raised his eyebrows and grinned. Hercules the wall painter was a small man with round shoulders, a bald head and a weak chin.

Flavia nodded.

"When I came downstairs, I found him making these sketches and when I asked him what he was going to paint he said . . . well, see for yourself."

Jonathan looked at the scenes sketched on the white wall.

"The first one shows a naked man wrestling a lion," said Jonathan, "and in the next one the naked man has obviously won because now he's wearing the lion skin and . . . Great Jupiter's eyebrows! It's Hercules!"

Flavia nodded. "Hercules the wall painter is painting the twelve tasks of Hercules the hero. As signs go, it couldn't be much clearer."

Lupus nodded.

"Flavia," said Nubia. "If you are never having babies, maybe your father should be having babies."

"But not with Cartilia."

Lupus shrugged at her, as if to ask: Why not?

"I just have a feeling." She looked around at them. "Anyway, I think that each task I complete will give me a clue and so by the end of my quest I'll know the truth. Yesterday—with Nubia's help—we beat the lion. Our next clue will be something to do with a hydra."

"But hydra is snake-headed dog," said Nubia.

"Where will we find one of those?" asked Jonathan.

Lupus held up his wax tablet:

# HYDRA FOUNTAIN

"Of course!" cried Jonathan. "In the part of town where we used to live, near the Marina Gate, there's a fountain called the hydra fountain. And there's an old lady who sits and spins wool nearby. They call her the Wise Woman of Ostia. Is that any good?"

"Perfect!" said Flavia. "Absolutely perfect."

■ ■ ■

Seven spouts of water gushed from seven serpents' heads at the hydra fountain. They found the old woman sitting nearby, on the porch of her house.

She was a tiny creature in black with a humped back and hands like claws. Her head was down, and patches of pink scalp showed through her thin white hair. A mass of gray wool was piled on a stool beside her and sleeping on top of it was a cat of the same color. The old woman was spinning the wool, and Nubia was fascinated to see the twist of gray yarn emerge from between her gnarled fingers.

"Hello," said Flavia politely. "Are you the Wise Woman of Ostia?"

The woman looked up at them sharply.

Nubia stifled a gasp. The old woman had one filmy gray eye and where the other should have been only an empty socket.

"No one is wise." Her voice was high and clear, like a child's. "But to some the gods give insight." She chuckled. "And others of us have just been around for a very long time."

"But are you the one they call the Wise Woman?"

"Some call me Lusca, because I have only one eye. Others call me Anus, because I was born the year Octavian was proclaimed Augustus."

Flavia gasped. "But that would make you . . ."

"More than a hundred years old," exclaimed Jonathan.

"Impossible!" snorted Flavia.

Nubia caught her breath. It was unimaginably rude to contradict a gray-hair. In Nubia's clan, the children were always taught to honor the old. So she stepped forward and clapped her hands together softly, letting her knees bend as she did so.

"Thank you, Nubia, for showing me respect."

"How did you know her name was Nubia?" gasped Flavia.

"I listen. People talk when they come to the hydra fountain here."

"Please," said Flavia. "May we ask you a question?"

60

"You may ask. But I may not answer."

Flavia reached for her coin purse. Nubia put a restraining hand on her arm, but Flavia shook it off. "I can pay you," she said. "One denarius."

With a sharp intake of breath, the old woman fixed her single eye on Flavia. "You think you can buy wisdom, Flavia Gemina? No! But because Nubia showed respect, I will answer one question."

"Thank you," said Flavia. "Can you please tell us where Cartilia—"

"A question of my own choosing!" said the Wise Woman.

Chastened, Flavia fell silent. Nubia held her breath and waited for a word of great wisdom.

"Cartilia Poplicola lives on Orchard Street," said the Wise Woman. "The house with the sky-blue door. You can't miss it: The knocker is in the shape of a club, like the one Hercules used to carry." The old woman held out a clawlike hand. "I'll have that bit of silver now."

"The third task of Hercules," said Flavia to the others, when they were out of the old woman's earshot, "was to capture the deer sacred to Diana. And I think we know who Diana is, don't we?"

Jonathan nodded. "Cartilia's sister."

"We know where she lives," said Flavia, stopping in front of the house with the club knocker. "But we can't just bang on the door and barge in. We need an excuse to visit. Luckily it's the Saturnalia. We can take Cartilia a gift and then they'll invite us in!"

"What are we giving her?" asked Nubia.

"I'm not sure. Traditionally on the Saturnalia you give a sigillum —one of those dolls—or silver or candles or food. . . . That's it! We'll raid the storeroom."

"While you're doing that," suggested Jonathan, "should Lupus and I attempt the fourth task?"

"Good idea," said Flavia. "Hercules' fourth task was to capture the Erymanthean Boar. Now where will we find a boar in Ostia?"

61

"Maybe we could go hunting?" said Jonathan hopefully.

Flavia gave him a sharp look. "You're not trying to get out of this, are you, Jonathan?"

"Of course not!"

Lupus snapped his fingers and wrote on his wax tablet:

## BRUTUS

"That's right," said Jonathan, "Lupus and I saw a huge boar outside the butcher's shop two days ago. They say he caught it himself."

"That sounds promising," said Flavia. "Brutus always has the latest gossip. You boys go there while Nubia and I take a jar of prunes to Cartilia. We'll meet back at my house at noon. All right?"

"Great," said Jonathan dryly. "A visit to the pork butcher's on the Sabbath. Father will be so pleased."

As Flavia banged the knocker on the sky-blue door, Nubia looked around. The shutters of the shops either side of Cartilia's house were pulled down, but music was coming from a tavern further down the road, and groups of rowdy people were spilling onto the street outside it.

"These houses are the oldest in Ostia," Flavia said to her. "Pater told me they were here even before the town wall was built."

It was beginning to rain. Nubia shivered and pulled Captain Geminus's old nutmeg-colored cloak tighter. Flavia banged the knocker again and glanced at Nubia.

"We'll just wait a little longer. The household slaves are probably down the road there at the Peacock Tavern."

Sure enough, a moment later they heard the scraping of the bolt and the door swung open. A tall woman with an elaborate hairstyle opened the door. Although there was no gray in her hair, Nubia guessed she was over forty.

"Hello, girls, may I help you?" she asked.

"Is this the house of Quintus Cartilius Poplicola?" asked Flavia politely, and held out the ceramic jar of prunes. "We've come to bring a Saturnalia gift for his daughter Cartilia."

The woman's face lit up. "How kind!" she said. "Which of my Cartilias do you mean: Diana or Paula?"

Nubia and Flavia exchanged a quick glance. "Paula," said Flavia.

"She's not here at the moment. . . ."The woman tipped her head to one side. "Am I correct in thinking you're Captain Geminus's daughter?"

"Yes." Flavia nodded. "My name is Flavia Gemina, and this is my friend Nubia."

"Then come in! I'm Paula's mother, Vibia."

She stood aside with a smile and beckoned the girls in. Nubia smiled back at Cartilia's mother as they moved through the vestibule. The woman's eyes were warm and kind, and although her complicated hairstyle was out of fashion it was still very impressive.

"My husband's not here right now," said Vibia. "He's entertaining his clients at the Forum of the Corporations. Both my daughters are out, and of course the slaves are out, too, celebrating the festival."

She led them through a bright, chilly atrium into a red-walled tablinum that smelled of cloves and parchment. Nubia went straight to the bronze tripod full of glowing coals and warmed her hands over it.

"Yes," said Vibia. "I feel the cold, too. This is my husband's study, but he won't mind us sitting here."

"Oh," said Flavia, going to an open scroll on the table. "He's been reading Apollodorus."

"No," said Vibia with a smile. "I have."

"The story of Diana?" asked Flavia, scanning the scroll.

"Yes. Hot spiced wine?"Vibia gestured toward a silver jug. Nubia nodded.

"Well-watered, thank you," said Flavia, and added, "I'm studying the myth of Hercules at the moment."

Vibia's face lit up as she poured the steaming wine into glossy black cups.

"My father claims Hercules as his ancestor," said Vibia. "Do please sit." She handed them their cups and added, "I find Hercules a very complex hero, and not always likeable."

Nubia sniffed the spicy wine and took a sip. It was nice: not too sweet and not too strong.

"I'm especially interested in the twelve tasks of Hercules," said Flavia.

Vibia nodded. "They say he had twelve but when you count up all his exploits, there were many more."

"Were there?" said Flavia with a look of dismay.

"Roast chestnuts!" cried Vibia.

"Hercules had to roast some chestnuts?"

"No, no. Let me roast you some chestnuts. My middle daughter used to love them but the rest of the family doesn't share my passion for them. I bought a basket of them last week and I've been waiting for someone to share them with." She put down her cup. "I'll only be a moment."

Vibia went out of the room. As soon as she was gone Flavia stood and wandered around the study, cup in hand, lightly touching the objects on the desk and reading the labels on the scrolls in their niches. Nubia looked around, too, but she remained in her chair, sipping her wine. The study, like so many in Ostia, had cinnabar-red walls and a few elegant pieces of furniture. A black-and-white mosaic floor was mostly hidden by a threadbare eastern carpet. It occurred to Nubia that this was the home of someone who had once been wealthy but could not afford to replace expensive items.

Vibia returned with a bowl of chestnuts and a sharp little kitchen knife.

Flavia glanced over from beside the scroll shelves and said, "I see you've got Euripides' play about Hercules."

"Yes," said Vibia, making an incision in one of the chestnuts and tossing it on the coals. "I love plays, and that's a particularly good one." She tossed another chestnut on the embers and smiled. "It does please me to meet a girl who is literate," she said. "I've tried to teach my three daughters the classics."

"Hello, Mater!"

Nubia turned her head to see a slim boy of about sixteen enter the study. He wore a short red tunic. In one hand he held a bow and in the other a brace of long-beaked woodcock.

"Hello, dear," said Vibia guardedly.

The boy slung the dead birds onto the desk and turned his long-lashed eyes on the girls. Nubia stared. She had never seen such a pretty boy. He had full lips and his tanned cheeks were smooth as marble. His short hair was brown and feathery, the same color as the birds' breasts.

Flavia was staring, too, at the boy's chest, and suddenly Nubia realized why.

"Girls," said Vibia, with a sigh, "I'd like you to meet my youngest daughter Cartilia, whom we call Diana."

# SCROLL XI

"Great Neptune's beard!" breathed Flavia. "You have short hair!"

She had never seen short hair on a freeborn girl before. She had read about it, knew that women often shaved their heads in extreme cases of grief or mourning, but to see a highborn girl with her head uncovered and a slave's haircut was shocking.

"Who did it to you?" she blurted out.

Diana turned her large brown eyes on Flavia and lifted her chin a fraction. "I did it to myself last month," she said. "I hate men and I never want to marry. I want to be like Diana, the virgin huntress."

Vibia smiled apologetically. "My daughter has radical beliefs," she said. "Spiced wine, dear?"

"No, thank you Mater, I'm just off to the tavern to meet my friends. Then I'm going hunting again."

"Dressed in that short little tunic?" said Vibia.

"Yes, Mater," said Diana coolly. "Dressed in this short little tunic."

"Any luck?" asked Flavia as she tipped the roasted chestnuts out of their papyrus cone onto the couch.

Jonathan took a chestnut and shook his head. "Sorry," he said. "We just stood around for an hour listening to all the men tell their wild boar stories."

Flavia peeled a chestnut. "I guess we need to find another boar."

It was noon and once again the four friends were sitting on one of the couches of her triclinium watching Hercules the wall painter. A brazier glowing in the center of the room did little to warm the cold air.

"He's very good," whispered Jonathan, nodding at the little man, who had his back to them.

Lupus nodded enthusiastically.

Hercules was dabbing his brush rapidly on the damp wall, applying the color before the plaster dried. He was painting the fourth task of Hercules. In this task, the hero was shown carrying a boar over his shoulders.

"Why is Hercules having no clothes?" asked Nubia. "Isn't he cold?"

"That shows he's a hero," explained Flavia. "A hero is someone who is half mortal and half divine. Remember? Hercules was the son of Jupiter."

"Yum," said Jonathan. "These chestnuts are delicious! Did you have any luck this morning?"

Flavia nodded. "We met Cartilia's younger sister Diana. She dresses like a boy and she has short hair!"

Lupus pointed at Nubia's head and raised his eyebrows.

"Yes, I know Nubia has short hair, but she used to be a slave and anyway it looks right on Nubia. Diana looked very strange."

Jonathan shelled another chestnut. "Does she look like a really pretty boy?"

"Exactly."

"Then I think I've seen her hunting in the woods once or twice. In Diana's Grove."

"That'll be her," said Flavia. "I'd love to know her story!"

Nubia sighed with pleasure.

She and Flavia had lingered in the pink marble sudatorium of the Baths of Atalanta for nearly an hour. Now she was standing over a drain with three leaf-shaped holes and scraping her skin with a bronze strigil.

At first she had found it strange–almost uncomfortable–scraping the oil-softened dead skin from her body, but now she hated to go more than a day or two without scraping down. With satisfaction, she watched the gray sludge drip from the strigil into the drain. In a minute she and Flavia would visit the cold plunge to wash off the residue, followed by a brisk rubdown with a towel. But first they always scraped each other's backs.

"Ready, Nubia?"

Nubia nodded and handed Flavia her strigil. Then she turned her back. Flavia had always done Nubia first, since the first day she had demonstrated how to use the strigil. In a moment, Nubia would return the favor. But for now she closed her eyes and enjoyed the sensation of having her back gently scraped.

Once again, Nubia sighed with pleasure.

Behind her Flavia laughed. "They say Romans love wine, the pleasure of Venus, and the baths, but you just love the baths!"

Nubia nodded happily. In the last month, she had learned the names of each of Ostia's twelve public baths. And over lunch she had remembered that one of them was called after the heroine who killed a foaming boar.

"This was a brilliant idea of yours to come to the Baths of Atalanta," said Flavia. "I've never been here before. They're so luxurious. . . ."

Located near the Marina Gate, the Baths of Atalanta were exclusively for women. All the frescoes and mosaics showed Atalanta beating men at various tasks. On the wall of the frigidarium, a frescoed Atalanta ran a race far ahead of her gasping male competitors. On the domed ceiling of the caldarium she smugly watched her father execute the suitors who had failed to win her hand in marriage. And here in the tepidarium—right at Nubia's feet—a black-and-white mosaic of Atalanta spearing a big, hairy boar while her male companions lay impotently around her.

Not only were the baths beautiful but so were the women who frequented them. Two exceptionally pretty women were oiling each other nearby. On the wall behind them was a fresco of Atalanta kissing Hippomenes, the youth who'd finally won her heart. It reminded Nubia of what she'd seen in the woods and she wondered again whether she should tell Flavia she had seen Aristo kissing a mysterious woman. But she found the words wouldn't come.

Behind her, Flavia stopped scraping.

"What?" Nubia turned her head.

"Shhh!" hissed Flavia, and put her mouth right in Nubia's ear. "Listen to them."

"Glycera only married him for his money," the redhead was saying. "She's already buried three husbands."

"I don't know how she does it," said the blonde. "Glycera's not half as pretty as you are. I simply don't see the attraction."

"They say," murmured the first woman, and Nubia had to strain to hear her words, "they say she's a witch, that she enchanted him."

"That would explain a lot," said the blonde in a less cautious tone of voice. "She uses one potion to win them and another to kill them off!"

"And then," said her friend, "she collects the legacy!"

# SCROLL XII

"And then," said Jonathan, "after he stopped screaming, he burst into tears. Imagine: a big old gladiator crying like a baby."

The four friends were having a conference at Jonathan's house before resuming their investigations.

"What was your father doing to him?" Flavia asked Jonathan. "Amputating a limb?"

He shook his head. "Just burning off a little mole. The gladiator said it spoiled his looks." Jonathan snorted as he spread some soft cheese on the flat bread. "And I'm telling you: That brute is not pretty."

Flavia's eyes opened wide. "Is he a famous gladiator? It wasn't Rodan, was it?"

"Taurus," said Jonathan. "He's called Taurus. He's here in Ostia, visiting his mother for the holidays."

"Wait!" cried Flavia. "His name isn't Taurus, is it?"

"That's what I just said."

"He's the one they call the Cretan Bull!"

Jonathan stared at her. "That's a coincidence."

"What coincidence?" asked Nubia.

"Hercules' seventh labor was to capture the Cretan bull," said Flavia, her gray eyes bright. "And Jonathan's father just treated a famous gladiator called the Cretan Bull!"

Lupus whistled softly.

Jonathan scratched his curly head. "Did you find out anything this afternoon?"

"Yes. Nubia had the brilliant idea of going to the Baths of Atalanta and we overheard someone talking about a woman who marries men and then poisons them to inherit their wealth."

"You don't think they were talking about Cartilia, do you?" asked Jonathan.

"No. The woman they were talking about was called Glycera and she was on her fourth husband. But apparently it's quite common. Women marry rich men, then kill them off. Or vice versa."

Lupus wrote something on his wax tablet.

## BUT YOUR FATHER ISN'T RICH

"I know," said Flavia. "But just between us, he's trying to give the impression we are. Maybe Cartilia thinks he's rich and wants to marry him for his money and then kill him off."

"Whoa!" said Jonathan. "You think Cartilia's only after your father's money? And that she's going to murder him for his inheritance?"

Flavia nodded. "But I admit we need more proof. We've got to continue our investigations. We've completed the first four tasks: the lion, the hydra, the deer, and the boar. Hercules' fifth labor was to clean the stables."

"Stables?" said Nubia, her eyes lighting up.

"Yes," said Flavia, "King Augeus had some stables. The fifth task of Hercules was to clean them out, because nobody had bothered for ten years."

Lupus grimaced and held his nose.

Flavia giggled. "Exactly. The poor horses were up to their noses in it."

Jonathan grinned. "Can I tell Nubia how he completed the task?"

71

"Of course."

"Hercules wasn't just strong," said Jonathan, turning to Nubia. "He was clever, too. In the hills above the stables was a stream. Hercules put a huge boulder in the stream and diverted the water down the hillside. Then he opened the front doors and the back doors of the stables. The water swept through and washed all the dung away!"

"Clever," said Nubia.

"Shouldn't we investigate Taurus the Cretan Bull before we go around the stables?" asked Jonathan.

"No," said Flavia. "I think we should complete the tasks in order. Capturing the Cretan bull was Hercules' seventh task. We still haven't completed five and six."

"So we have to go and clean some stables this afternoon?" Jonathan raised an eyebrow.

"Hopefully we won't have to clean them, just visit them," said Flavia. She sucked a strand of her light brown hair thoughtfully. "There are two stables in Ostia. Any idea which one has the most dung?"

They all looked at Lupus.

He gave them his bug-eyed "What?" expression, then snapped his fingers and nodded.

"I knew Lupus would have the answer," laughed Flavia. They leaned in to watch him write:

# HEAD SLAVE AT
# LAURENTUM GATE STABLES
# IS CALLED FIMUS

Flavia laughed again. "That's it then. Shall we go?"

"Wait," said Jonathan. "The sixth task of Hercules was to kill the Stymphalian birds, wasn't it?"

"Correct," said Flavia.

72

"Well," said Jonathan, nudging Lupus, "apparently the ostrich was spotted in the woods this morning. Aristo invited Lupus and me to go hunting with him this afternoon. The magistrate declared all the escaped animals fair game, so Aristo and some friends are going to try to catch it."

"Perfect! That's my Stymphalian bird! You two don't mind going, do you?"

"Do we mind hunting instead of trailing around the stables after you?"

Jonathan and Lupus glanced at each other.

"Not at all," said Jonathan with a grin.

"There's definitely something strange about those Poplicola girls," said Fimus the stable slave. He was a potbellied man with a blotched face and infected eyes.

Nubia averted her eyes from his unpleasant face and inhaled. The Laurentum Gate stables smelled nice—a mixture of hay and horses and dung. It was warm, here, too. Nubia knew that whenever Flavia's father or uncle needed to hire a horse, this was where they came.

"What's strange about the Poplicola girls?" asked Flavia.

A chestnut-colored mare put her head over one of the stall doors and nickered softly. Nubia moved over to the stall and let the mare sniff her hand.

"The Poplicola women all ride," Fimus said. "It's not often you see a woman on horseback. Barbaric, if you ask me."

Nubia stroked the mare's nose. She didn't think there was anything strange about a woman riding a horse. All the women in her clan could ride a horse as well as a camel.

"Also," said Fimus, "one of them's just gone and cut off all her hair."

"Diana," said Flavia.

"Is that her name?" Fimus frowned. "I thought it was something else."

"Diana's just her nickname," said Flavia. "She and her sisters are all called Cartilia."

"Oh," said the slave. "Well, anyway, the women in that family aren't quite right, if you ask me. Their mother rides, too."

"Vibia?" said Flavia.

"That's her."

"Can you tell us anything else about that family?"

"Paula! That's her name. She's the strange one. She came in here last week, asking about that gladiator."

"Who? Taurus the Cretan Bull?"

"That's him. He's spending the holidays here in Ostia."

"I know. And Paula asked where he lived?"

"No," said Fimus, scratching his belly. "That's the strange thing. She asked which baths he usually went to."

Aristo's friend Lysander was a short dark Greek employed by the corporation of grain measurers as a scribe and accountant. But today he had put aside his abacus and wax tablets to enjoy a day of hunting.

"Can you boys make a lot of noise?" he asked Jonathan and Lupus. "All the slaves are on holiday and we need some beaters."

"Of course," said Jonathan. Lupus nodded vigorously and started howling.

"Not yet!" Lysander rolled his eyes. "We have to set up the net first."

They were standing near the tomb of Avita Procula near the Grove of Diana. The afternoon was cold but the wind had died and a high cloud cover gave the world an unreal, pearly glow.

"Let's go then," said Aristo.

"We're just waiting for one more person," said Lysander, flushing.

Aristo gave Lysander a sharp look. "Don't tell me you've invited her!"

"I'm sorry, Aristo. But she asked to come. And you know how I feel about her. . . ."

"By the gods, Lysander! Now she's going to think I—"

"Shhh!" Lysander hissed. "Here she comes."

Lupus heard Aristo curse under his breath and he saw Jonathan's eyes open wide. He turned to see a boy striding confidently toward them from the direction of the Laurentum Gate. He wore a red tunic and red leather boots. A short cloak of moss-green wool was slung over his shoulders and in his right hand he carried a hunting javelin.

Lupus frowned and as the boy drew nearer he saw it was not a boy at all, but a girl with unnaturally short hair.

Jonathan bent his head and whispered in Lupus's ear, "Diana."

Lupus nodded. And stared. Jonathan had called her pretty. Nobody had said she was beautiful.

# SCROLL XIII

"I'm afraid I can't let you girls in," said Oleosus, the door slave at the Forum Baths. "Men only today. . . ." He was a loose-limbed youth with floppy black hair and heavy-lidded brown eyes.

"But we just saw two women come in," protested Flavia. "One of them was wearing a pink mantle and the other was holding a waxed parasol."

"Oh, them." Oleosus gave them a lazy smile. "The senator's daughters. They've just come to watch Taurus training. And for some of his scrapings."

"For some *what?*"

"Some of his scrapings. After he's worked up a sweat, his slave scrapes him down. Then he puts the . . . er . . . mixture in cheap little bottles and sells it to the ladies. They pay a gold coin per bottle."

*"What?"* Flavia's jaw dropped. *"Why?"*

He winked. "They say if you mix a little in someone's food—"

"In their *food?*"

He nodded. "Mix a little in someone's food and he'll become very passionate and desire you."

"A love potion!" Flavia breathed.

She and Nubia glanced at each other.

"Does it work?" Flavia asked him.

Oleosus shrugged. "It works for Taurus. They say he just bought his mother a nice little farm with the money he's made from his scrapings."

"And respectable women buy the scrapings?"

"All sorts of women buy it."

"I don't suppose you remember any of their names?" Flavia toyed with the pouch tied to her belt, so that the coins clinked softly. "A woman named Cartilia Poplicola, for example?"

He frowned.

"A little taller than me?" prompted Flavia. "About twenty-five? Pretty in a cold sort of way? Calls herself Paula?"

His face relaxed into a smile. "Oh, Paula!" he said. "She came around as soon as he arrived in town. Bought a jar last week and another one yesterday!"

As they set up the net, Lupus couldn't stop looking at Diana.

He noticed that Lysander was watching her, too, and saw a wounded look in his eyes. Glancing back at Diana, Lupus saw the reason. She had bent down to whisper something in Aristo's ear. Her fingers, resting lightly on the back of his neck, toyed with his curls in a gesture of startling intimacy.

Aristo, intent on anchoring the net to the ground, did not even raise his eyes to look at her. Lupus saw his jaw clench and suddenly he realized what was happening.

Lysander loved Diana, but she loved Aristo. And it was obvious that Aristo despised her. Lupus snorted as he tied one of the red feathers to the edge of the net: Cupid the love god was such a mischief maker.

"So, Diana," said Jonathan, "you're Paula's sister."

"What?" Diana scowled at him, then stood up.

"Cartilia Paula is your sister," repeated Jonathan.

Diana nodded curtly and moved forward to inspect one of the fastenings on the net.

"Is she nice?"

Diana pouted. "No. She's a greedy old witch."

"Oh. Sorry to upset you."

"Don't mention her and I won't be upset."

"Right then." Jonathan whistled a little tune, then gave Lupus a significant look.

When the net was securely fixed between some trees, and its edge marked with red feathers, the five of them moved quietly back through the grove, scanning the soft ground for any sign of their prey.

Lupus pretended to look for ostrich tracks, too, but he was really watching Diana out of the corner of his eye. His alertness paid off. When they were almost out of the grove, Lysander knelt to examine something near a tiny stream.

"Here," said Lysander, pointing at the mud. "That's the footprint of an ostrich."

As they all gathered round to look, Lupus saw Diana slip something into Aristo's belt. A piece of papyrus.

"It's fresh!" said Jonathan.

As they all peered down at it, Lupus saw Aristo's hand close over the note.

"This must be where the creature comes to drink," said Lysander, standing up again and looking around. "I think the bird was here this morning and he may well return tomorrow." He glanced up at the sky. "It's getting late. I suggest we make an early start tomorrow—maybe bring some dogs. We'll start over there at the edge of the grove and beat toward the net. Agreed?"

The others nodded.

"Can you boys bring something noisy? Castanets, rattles, tambourines? There are only a few of us so we'll have to make a lot of noise."

As they walked back toward the town walls, Lupus saw Aristo unfold the scrap of papyrus that Diana had slipped him.

Aristo scanned the note, then crushed it into a ball and let it drop to the muddy ground.

"So we'll meet tomorrow just past dawn?" said Diana a few minutes later. They stood at the fork in the road. Diana was looking at Aristo but it was Lysander who replied.

"That's right," he said. "At the tomb of Avita Procula. Same place we met today." Lysander nodded toward the Laurentum Gate, "Are you going home now, Diana? Shall I walk with you?"

"No," said Diana over her shoulder. "I'm going to make an offering to the goddess and ask her to give me success in the hunt."

I think I know what you're hunting, thought Lupus.

And later, back in his room, when he smoothed out her papyrus note, he saw that his suspicion had been correct.

"Scrapings," said Flavia to Jonathan. "The door slave at the Forum Baths told us that if you mix some of a gladiator's sweaty scrapings in someone's food then that person will fall in love with you."

"Ewww,'" said Jonathan and then frowned. "But how can you be sure the person falls in love with you? I mean, wouldn't he fall in love with the gladiator? Or the first person he sees? Because that never works. At least not in the plays. . . ."

"No," said Flavia. "Before you put it in their food you say a kind of prayer over the mixture. To Venus. And then—here's the really disgusting bit—you spit in it. Or put some of your other bodily fluids in."

"And again I say: ewww." Jonathan shuddered. He was at Flavia's house, leaning against the warm kitchen wall and watching the girls prepare dinner. Nubia was stirring a pot of stew and Flavia was cutting up some firm white mushrooms. When she reached for another handful Jonathan grabbed some slices from the chopping board. They were delicious.

"Apparently," said Flavia, "when the person eats the food with the potion in it, they have a gladiator's passion for whoever spat in the potion. And that's why Cartilia wanted the gladiator's scrapings. She has obviously bewitched Pater! I told Nubia the first day I saw her. I said, 'I'll bet she's bewitched Pater.' Didn't I, Nubia?"

"Yes," said Nubia and continued to stir the stew.

Jonathan popped a slice of mushroom in his mouth. "And the slave at the baths said she bought some of Taurus's scrapings?"

Flavia nodded. "Twice. About a week ago and yesterday."

She slapped Jonathan's hand as it crept forward to take another mushroom.

"So you think she's already put some of this disgusting love potion in your father's food?" he asked.

"Yes. They saw each other a few days ago at Cordius's house. I think she must have done it then. Maybe mixed it in his spiced wine or something. Remember I told you he seemed different? That morning we ran away from the ostrich?"

"Yes," said Jonathan.

Flavia pushed the mushroom slices to one side of the chopping board and removed some leeks from the bowl of salted water.

"Speaking of ostriches," she said, as she began to slice the leeks, "how did you get on today? Any luck?"

"No," said Jonathan. "The ostrich wasn't in the woods. But we saw a fresh footprint and we've set a trap for it. A big net with red feathers at the edges. Lysander says the animals avoid the feathers and run straight into the center of the net. Tomorrow we'll beat the woods and drive the ostrich into it. If he's there, that is."

"I meant did you get any more information about Cartilia?"

"Actually we did. Cartilia's sister was helping us set up the net." Flavia stopped slicing. "Diana was hunting with you?"

Jonathan nodded. "And she called Cartilia a greedy old witch."

"I knew it!" said Flavia, putting down her knife. "What else did she say?"

"Nothing. She went all pouty when I mentioned Cartilia."

"Do you think you can milk her for more information?"

"I don't know," said Jonathan. "She doesn't like talking about her sister." Seeing the expression on Flavia's face, he added, "Lupus and I are going hunting with them tomorrow at dawn. We'll try to get more information then."

"Good!" Flavia resumed her chopping. "Where did you say Lupus was?"

"Running an errand for Father. He volunteered to go into town and deliver some ointment to one of Father's patients. He shouldn't be long."

Lupus hid behind a column and waited until the group of drunken revelers had passed by on their way home from the tavern. Then he looked at the scrap of papyrus again. He was glad he had learned how to read. Only a few months ago the black marks would have meant nothing to him. Now they made his heart pound with excitement.

# MEET ME BEHIND THE SHRINE OF THE CROSSROADS AT DUSK. WE MUST TALK. FROM CARTILIA.

Lupus could barely see the letters in the fading light. Soon it would be dark. He had delivered the doctor's medicine and now he was waiting to see whether Aristo would meet Diana at the shrine.

Ostia's main street was almost deserted now. Only one or two drunken slaves wandered about, trying to remember where they lived. Lupus pressed his back to the column as a pair of vigiles strolled past. Both held torches. One had a large water skin slung over his back, the other carried a thick hemp mat rolled up on his shoulders. Lupus knew their job was to patrol the town to prevent crime and especially fire, a particular danger during the winter when braziers, oil lamps, and torches burned in every home.

The men passed by without seeing him and Lupus felt a slow

smile spread across his face. He had missed the excitement of the hunt. Of becoming invisible. Of watching people who thought they were alone.

After the vigiles turned the corner, Lupus ran silently along the murky colonnade until he reached the end. Then, like a shadow, he quickly descended the three steps and slipped through the forum. Crouching low, he moved toward the shrine of the crossroads, glad of his silent new boots.

The thickening purple gloom of dusk blanketed the town now. He could see a single yellow lamp flickering somewhere inside the shrine and the black silhouettes of two cypress trees rising up behind it. Somewhere a blackbird uttered its warning cry in the cold air. He could smell the winter smell of wood smoke.

As he started to make his way to the back of the marble shrine, he tripped on something and fell onto the damp ground.

He could barely make out the dark form lying beside the shrine.

Tentatively, Lupus reached out and touched it.

It was the body of a man.

# SCROLL XIV

His heart pounding, Lupus recoiled from the body. It was still warm.

The body groaned.

He was still alive!

Then Lupus caught the rancid odor of vomit and he turned away with mixed relief and disgust. It was only a reveler who had passed out after drinking too much spiced wine.

He stood up again and his fingertips on the cold marble wall guided him around the back of the shrine. He sensed rather than saw the two trees ahead of him.

Suddenly, in the darkness, he heard a woman's voice, low and urgent.

"Aristo?" said the voice. "Aristo, is that you?"

Lupus pressed himself against the trunk of one of the trees and held his breath.

"Aristo?" repeated the voice.

Lupus's heart was pounding so loudly he was sure she must be able to hear it. The crunch of her foot on a twig alerted him and he moved around the trunk, keeping it between them.

"Aristo? Stop playing games with me. . . ."

Silence.

"I know you're there. I can hear you breathing."

Lupus tipped his head back and closed his eyes, listening with all his might: ready to move one way if she moved the other.

"Why are you doing this to me? Why are you torturing me? Aristo, I love you. I love you so much. . . ."

From the road a flicker of lamplight and the crunch of military boots on paving stones. Another pair of vigiles were approaching.

Lupus heard the woman curse softly and move away.

After a moment he heard a man's deep voice. "Hey, miss. You shouldn't be out after dark. This is a favorite hiding place for robbers."

"Can we escort you home?" said the other watchman.

"Yes . . . yes please!" Her voice was trembling.

It was easy to follow her after that. The flickering torches lit the three figures as they moved down the center of the road: the woman between the two big watchmen.

Once she turned to look back, but Lupus quickly pressed himself into the inky black shadows of a storefront.

Presently, as he had expected, they stopped in front of Cartilia's house. He heard the brass knocker resound and saw a path of light pour out from within as the door opened almost immediately. There were relieved voices and the woman stepped inside.

Lupus was almost certain the woman had been Diana. But he was not positive: She had worn a long cloak, and a hood that covered her face.

Nubia held her hands over the glowing coals and rubbed them together. It was just before dawn on the third day of the Saturnalia. The dogs were snuffling in the dark garden, eager to be off for the hunt. The four friends stood in the kitchen, warming themselves by the hearth while Lupus and Jonathan waited for Aristo to come out of the latrine. Captain Geminus and the slaves were still asleep.

"You're sure Aristo was here yesterday at dusk?" Jonathan whispered.

Flavia nodded. "He came in right after you left. He'd caught some rabbits and we put them in the stew. Why do you ask?"

Jonathan lowered his voice even more: "Yesterday, while we were setting up the net, Lupus saw Diana slip Aristo a note. She wanted him to meet her at the shrine of the crossroads. She came to the shrine but he never appeared."

"Why did she want to meet him in such a strange place at such a strange time?"

"We think she's in love with him," said Jonathan.

Nubia felt a strange sensation in the pit of her stomach.

"Cartilia's sister loves Aristo?" Flavia's eyes opened wide.

Lupus nodded emphatically and wrote on his tablet.

# LYSANDER LOVES DIANA.
# DIANA LOVES ARISTO.
# BUT ARISTO DOESN'T LIKE DIANA.

"Who is Lysander?" asked Nubia.

"He's Aristo's Greek friend," said Jonathan. "Short. Dark. They often hunt together."

"It's the classic love triangle," said Flavia, nodding wisely.

"Why triangle?" asked Jonathan.

"Well, A loves B and B loves C. It's a triangle."

"No it's not," said Jonathan. "It's a V. If C loves A, then it's a triangle."

"Good point." Flavia turned to Lupus. "How did you know what Diana's note said?" she asked him.

Lupus presented the scrap of papyrus with a flourish.

Flavia grabbed the note and held it close to the red hearth coals so she could read it. Nubia peered over her shoulder.

"But it's signed Cartilia." Flavia frowned and straightened up. "Are you sure it was Diana who came to the shrine?"

Lupus looked at her. Then he shrugged.

# SHE WAS WEARING LONG CLOAK

he wrote on his tablet.

"Gray cloak with hood?" whispered Nubia.

Lupus nodded and gave her his bug-eyed look.

"How did you know what she was wearing?" asked Flavia.

They all looked at Nubia.

She took a breath. "Two days after Miriam's betrothal . . ."

"The first day of the Saturnalia?" asked Flavia.

Nubia nodded. "On that afternoon when I take the dogs in woods, behold! I see Aristo and woman in cloak."

"What were they doing?" asked Jonathan.

Nubia felt her face grow hot. "Kissing. Very kissing."

"Great Juno's peacock," whispered Flavia. "Why didn't you tell us this before?"

Nubia hung her head. She herself wasn't sure why she hadn't mentioned it.

"It doesn't matter," said Flavia. "But who was she? Did you see her face?"

Nubia shook her head and looked up at Flavia. "No. I did not see her face. She was wearing cloak. Gray cloak with hood."

# SCROLL XV

"Man-eating horses," said Flavia. "Where will we find man-eating horses in Ostia?"

"Stables?" suggested Nubia.

"I suppose we could try the Laurentum Gate stables again. Or the other ones: the Cart Drivers' stables. . . ." Flavia's voice trailed off.

It was an hour past dawn. The boys and Aristo had gone off to hunt their ostrich and once again the two girls were sitting on a dust-sheet–covered couch in the dining room. They were sipping milky spiced wine and watching Hercules prepare the last wall. He was using a wide brush to cover the old mustard-yellow plaster with a thin coat of lime mixed with plaster. When this dried it would make a brilliant base for the new images.

"We need to find mad horses," said Flavia. "Or maybe someone called Diomedes. That was the name of their master. He used to feed chopped-up people to his horses. That's what drove his horses mad. So Hercules completed the labor by killing Diomedes and feeding him to his own horses. Then they were so full and sleepy that Hercules was easily able to capture them."

"In baths?" said Nubia hopefully. "Maybe mosaics of man-eating horses in baths."

"I don't know of any," said Flavia.

"There's a retired legionary named Diomedes," said Hercules the wall painter. "New in town. Belongs to one of those new religions."

"What?" cried Flavia. "What did you just say?" It was the first time she had heard him speak.

Hercules turned to look at them. His watery eyes twinkled and his rubbery mouth curved in a smile.

"Diomedes," he said in a squeaky voice. "He's a retired soldier and he's the priest of a new cult. They worship a young god who was born near the end of December. Once a week his followers gather to share bread and wine, in order to remember the last supper he ate before he ascended to a higher plane."

"Oh," said Flavia. "Diomedes must be a Christian. They worship a shepherd named Jesus. They call him the Christ or Messiah."

"No," said Hercules, dipping his brush in the whitewash mixture, "Diomedes certainly isn't a Christian; I would know. The name of his god is something else. Starts with M . . . Menecrates? Marsyas? Mithras? That's it. Diomedes is a priest of Mithras. He lives not far from here, in a house just off Fuller's Street. I often pass that way. I see them gathering to observe their special meal on Sunday mornings."

"But it's Sunday morning now!"

"Yes it is," said Hercules. "If you hurry, you might catch them. . . ."

"My dear boys," said Lysander. "What are you doing with bows and arrows? You know we're using the net today. And I've got my hunting spear."

"Oh, leave them alone," said Aristo. "We may never catch this ostrich and at least they might bring home a rabbit or two."

"Very well," Lysander sighed. "You boys need to move slowly toward the net. Let the dogs bark and make as much noise as you can. Can you count as high as three hundred?"

Lupus nodded. Nipur was tugging at his lead, but Lupus was

strong enough to hold him. Jonathan was in charge of Tigris and Aristo held Scuto. The three dogs were wheezing with eagerness to be off.

"Good," said Lysander. "Don't start beating till you've reached three hundred. That will give me time to take up position by the net."

"What?" said Jonathan. "You're going to sit by the net while the rest of us do all the work?"

"That's the way it works," said Lysander with a grin. "Diana, would you like to join me?"

"Why don't you stay with the boys?" Diana said to Lysander. "Aristo and I can wait by the net."

Lysander's grin faded and Aristo looked up sharply.

"Er . . . no," he said. "I'm the boys' tutor. It's my job to protect them. I'll stay with them. Diana, you wait by the net with Lysander."

Diana turned wounded brown eyes on Aristo. For a moment their gazes locked. Aristo looked away first, guiltily it seemed to Lupus.

Diana turned on her heel. "Come on then, Lysander!" she snapped over her shoulder. "Let's go."

Diomedes, priest of Mithras, stood in his open doorway and gazed down at Flavia. Although he was quite an old man—in his early fifties—he was still lean and muscular.

"Cartilia Poplicola," she repeated. The stench of urine from the nearby fullers was so strong that Flavia had to breathe through her mouth.

Diomedes snorted. "Don't mention that woman to me! Her husband Caldus was one of our new initiates. But he's not with us any more." Diomedes shook his head angrily. "And it's her fault," he muttered.

Flavia's eyes opened wide. "It was her fault?"

"That's what I was told." He frowned. "I'm sorry," he said. "What did you say your name was?"

"Flavia Gemina, daughter of Marcus Flavius Geminus, sea captain."

"I don't know the name. Is he one of our followers?"

"No, I just—"

"Young lady. I am very busy today. I thought you were bringing a message from one of our members. That's why I opened the door to you. May I ask you to come back later?"

"That's all right," said Flavia politely. "I won't bother you again. Thank you very much. You've just told me what I needed to know."


Jonathan shook his tambourine with one hand and gripped Tigris's lead in the other. They were moving slowly through the pine grove making as much noise as possible. Over on his right, Lupus was beating his goatskin drum.

"Steady, Tigris!" called Jonathan, feeling the tug on the lead. "We want to take it slowly. Give the big bird time to hear us coming. . . ."

He glanced at Aristo, just visible through the trees on his left. Aristo held Scuto's taut lead and occasionally he clattered some castanets.

Jonathan looked up. It was morning now, with a high clear sky that would deepen to blue as the day progressed. He sucked in a lungful of air, as cold and intoxicating as the snow-chilled wine he had tasted once at a rich man's house. It was good to be out in the woods hunting with his friends and the dogs.

Hunting helped him forget the worries that were as constant as the throbbing of the brand on his left arm.

Worries about how he and his father would cope when Miriam was married and living in Laurentum. Worries about Lupus, who occasionally still disappeared without a word. Worries about Aristo, who seemed so distracted lately. Worries about Flavia, who was becoming exactly what she had sworn not to become: a tyrant.

And the biggest worry of all, the subject that was always there, drawing his thoughts toward Rome. . . .

"Jonathan! Look out!"

Aristo's voice clear across the glade and a crashing from the thicket ahead and there was the ostrich. The bird seemed confused by the din and in spite of Tigris's hysterical barking it took a flapping step toward Jonathan.

Jonathan lifted his tambourine and gave it a shake. "Go the other way, you stupid ostrich," he muttered. "The other way! Toward the net!"

But the ostrich didn't understand Latin.

It charged straight at him.

# SCROLL XVI

Jonathan reacted by instinct. He dropped the tambourine and Tigris's lead. In one fluid motion he lifted the bow from across his body with his left hand and plucked an arrow from his quiver with the right. There was no need to take careful aim. The enormous flapping bird was almost upon him.

Jonathan fired straight into its chest and then threw himself out of the way.

The ostrich's forward momentum carried it past and Jonathan lifted himself—gasping—on one muddy elbow. He was just in time to see the creature swerve toward Aristo, who threw his javelin.

The bird flapped, staggered, then veered again to receive a second arrow—this one in the neck—from Lupus's bow. Now the dogs were upon it and Jonathan was almost sorry as he watched them bring the bird heavily to the ground.

"Get the dogs away," cried Aristo. "The feathers are worth a fortune!"

Jonathan had trained the puppies well; they obeyed his command immediately and quickly backed away. But Scuto wanted to play with the giant thrashing bird. Suddenly one of the ostrich's powerful legs caught Flavia's dog in the chest. With a yelp, Scuto went flying through the air and Jonathan heard the terrible thud as he fell.

Aristo ran forward, hunting knife in hand, and stamped hard on the bird's neck just below the head. Then, with one swift, slashing movement, he ended the creature's misery.

Jonathan ran to Scuto. Flavia's dog lay motionless in the mud and pine needles. Nipur and Tigris were sniffing him and whimpering, and Lupus already had his ear against Scuto's chest.

Jonathan stopped and looked down at Lupus. "Is he . . . Is he dead?"

Doctor Mordecai lifted his head from the patient and smiled. "He's going to be all right. He may possibly have cracked a rib or two, but there's not much we can do. He just needs to rest until it heals." Scuto lay panting quietly on Flavia's bed.

"Oh, Doctor Mordecai!" Flavia threw her arms around Mordecai's waist and squeezed. "Thank you! Did you hear that?" She turned to the others and the look on her face made them all smile, even Aristo.

"We have to celebrate tonight!" Flavia cried. "Alma, I know it's the Saturnalia, and I'm supposed to be cooking but I want to nurse Scuto back to health and would you mind?"

"My dear, I'd like nothing better!" cried Alma. "We'll chop up that big bird and eat him for weeks."

"Wait!" said Jonathan. "We can't just go chopping it up. Aren't we supposed to share it out with Lysander and Diana?"

"Dear Apollo!" cried Aristo. "I'd forgotten all about them." He glanced out through the latticework screen of the window. "It's almost noon. I hope they haven't been sitting out there this whole time! I'd better go tell them. Lysander will be furious."

Lupus snorted and Jonathan nodded his agreement, "He's not the only one."

Lupus loved oysters.

They were cool and slippery and he could easily swallow them whole. He often had good dreams after eating them, and he was always full of energy the following day.

93

And so he was delighted when Alma set a plate of oysters before his couch.

It was midafternoon on the third day of the Saturnalia. They were celebrating the capture of the ostrich and Scuto's survival. Lupus reclined next to Jonathan and Mordecai. On the couch opposite him were Aristo, Flavia, and Nubia. Flavia's father and Cartilia Poplicola shared the central couch.

Flavia had been in a good mood when she handed them their garlands of ivy and mistletoe. She didn't even seem to mind Cartilia's presence. Lupus saw the reason at once: Scuto lay in his usual place under the central couch.

Flavia's father was in a good mood, too. He'd spent the day with his twin brother Gaius a few miles down the coast at Laurentum. Gaius's landlord, a young man named Pliny, had sent a Saturnalia gift of three dozen fresh oysters in a cask of seawater.

## OYSTERS ARE MY FAVORITE

Lupus wrote on his wax tablet and held it up for all to see.

"Oh! What a good idea!" cried Flavia. "Let's all say what our favorite food is! As king of the Saturnalia, I command it! Mine is roast chicken. And salad. What about you, Jonathan?"

"Venison stew," he said, "especially if I caught the deer myself."

"I love mushrooms," said Aristo.

"Me, too," said Jonathan.

"My favorite food is salted tuna," said Flavia's father. He laughed. "How about you, Cartilia?"

"I love salads," she said. "But I also adore oysters. The first time I—"

"Next!" cried Flavia. "What about you, Doctor Mordecai?"

After a short hesitation and a glance at Cartilia, Mordecai said softly, "I am very partial to lamb. Roast lamb in particular."

Flavia turned to Nubia and laughed. "And I think we all know Nubia's favorite food. . . ."

"Dates!" they all cried together, and Nubia smiled.

"Yes," she said. "I am loving dates. But now I am loving them even more with almond inside."

"And that brings us back to Lupus and the oysters!" said Flavia. "Let's eat!"

Lupus reached for the tiny glass jug of vinegar. He dribbled a few drops onto the first of his oysters.

The oyster twitched.

Lupus grunted with approval. Using his spoon, he freed the oyster from its shell, tipped his head back and let it slip down his throat. Then he tossed the shell into the center of the room. It fell with a clatter onto the marble floor. Nipur trotted forward, sniffed it, then sneezed. Scuto yawned and remained where he was. He knew oyster shells weren't edible.

Lupus grinned. And tested the next oyster.

"Why are you putting vinegar on him?" asked Nubia.

"To see if it's still alive," said Cartilia. "Right, Lupus?"

Lupus gave her a thumbs-up. Then he tipped his head back and swallowed the second oyster.

"They're still alive?" Jonathan had been examining an oyster. Now he hastily put it back on the plate and stared at it suspiciously.

"Try it, Jonathan!" said Cartilia. "Drop a little vinegar on the oyster. If it contracts, that means it's still alive. They're very good for you, aren't they doctor?"

Mordecai nodded. "I always recommend them for pregnant mothers and invalids. The fresher the better."

Lupus grinned as Jonathan dribbled some vinegar from the cruet onto his oyster.

"Ahh!" Jonathan started back. "It moved! It is alive. I'm not eating that!"

"Come on, Jonathan!" cried Flavia. "They're good for you."

"I don't want something alive crawling around inside me!"

"They can't crawl," laughed Cartilia. "They have no feet."

Lupus showed Jonathan his wax tablet.

# CAN I HAVE YOUR SHARE THEN?

"Jonathan," said Mordecai. "It is extremely impolite to refuse a host's food."

"All right," sighed Jonathan. "I'll try one."

"Just free it from its shell," said Cartilia.

"It's attached by a little sucker," explained Aristo.

"And swallow it down whole!" said Flavia.

"Shouldn't I chew it?" asked Jonathan, not taking his eyes from the gray blob glistening in its shell.

"No!" they all cried.

"Don't think about what you're eating," said Cartilia. "Just do it."

Jonathan hesitated.

"Jonathan!" said Flavia firmly. "As king of the Saturnalia I command you to eat that oyster!"

Everyone laughed and Jonathan gave them a queasy smile. Finally he took a deep breath, tipped back his head, and bravely swallowed it whole.

Everyone laughed again at the expression on Jonathan's face and Lupus inclined his head in thanks as his friend grimly slid the plate of oysters toward him.

Flavia was in the latrine when she heard the first chords of Aristo's lyre and the warble of Nubia's flute.

She smiled. It was a new song Nubia had written for Aristo. She called it "The Storyteller." Flavia heard the beat of Lupus's drum and thought how much he'd improved in the past month. Then Jonathan came in on his barbiton, a steady thrum so low you hardly heard it, but missed if it wasn't there.

Flavia quickly finished her business and put the sponge stick back in the beaker of vinegar. They needed her. It wasn't right without the tambourine.

She opened the door of the latrine and stepped out. Then she froze.

The tambourine had just joined the other instruments, strong, steady, confident. And much better than she ever played it. Flavia took a step forward and looked through the ivy-twined columns toward the dining room.

It was late: Dusk was approaching. Beyond the blue-green garden, the dining room looked like an illuminated treasure box. A dozen oil lamps filled the room with golden light and the two freshly painted walls glowed red. Jonathan was wearing his cinnamon caftan. Lupus wore his sea-green tunic and a Saturnalia cap he had found somewhere; it was red felt, trimmed with white fur. Flavia could hear Nubia and Aristo; she didn't need to see them. But she needed to know who was playing her part. She took another step forward and swallowed hard as the central couch came into view and she saw who was banging her tambourine.

It was Cartilia. Cartilia had taken her place.

For several days a particular sequence of notes—with what Aristo called a key change—had been sounding over and over in Nubia's head. It was a passage where her flute and Aristo's lyre played the notes above a strong deep beat of drum and barbiton, and a jingle of tambourine. Nubia had been craving the sound of it as she sometimes craved the taste of salt on bread. Now they were playing the song and the sequence was coming up. She could barely contain her excitement.

She was here. Sitting cross-legged on the foot of the couch. In this red and gold room. About to hear and play the music she had been longing for. The anticipation was delicious.

It was coming . . . coming . . . coming . . . and now!

As she played the key change, the notes inside her head fused with the notes outside her, notes so real that she physically felt them. Her body gave an involuntary shudder as they played the passage. How could that happen? How could you crave a melody as you craved a type of food? It was as if her heart had been hungry for the song.

97

Nubia turned her head as she played, and looked at her friends. Lupus, his head tipped to one side as he drummed away. And Jonathan, smiling up at her from his deep barbiton. Cartilia was a revelation, her eyes were closed and there was a sweet smile on her face as she shook the tambourine.

And Aristo—the storyteller—lost in the music. Nubia hadn't told him that the song was about him; she had been too shy. His curly head was down but she could see his thick eyelashes and as she watched his fingers moving swiftly over the strings, a huge wave of affection washed over Nubia. The music that had arisen in her heart now flowed back to her from him. He and the music were one. And because she loved the music, she loved him, too.

Suddenly her fingers were trembling too much to play. The notes of her flute hesitated, faltered, and failed. Her heart was pounding louder than Lupus's drum.

The others stopped playing, too, and the music died.

"Are you all right, Nubia?" Aristo looked concerned. Nubia nodded and dropped her flute and pressed her cool hands against her hot face.

Oh no, she thought. It can't be.

"Nubia?" It was Mordecai's voice. "What's the matter?"

"I am just feeling . . ." She knew they were all staring at her—that he was staring at her—and she couldn't bear it. Without looking at any of them, she slipped off the couch and ran out of the dining room.

Jonathan watched Nubia run out and opened his mouth to say something. But he closed it again as Flavia stalked in. Her face was pale as she went straight to the central couch and held out her hand.

"That's my tambourine," Flavia said to Cartilia. "Please give it to me."

"Flavia!" Captain Geminus's voice was angry but Cartilia answered calmly.

"I'm so sorry, Flavia. I didn't mean to take what was yours. Shall I bring my own next time?"

Jonathan saw the fury flicker in Flavia's eyes and he knew she was about to say something they would all regret.

"Aaaaah!" he yelled, and clutched his stomach. "Owwwwww!" He writhed realistically on the couch, careful not to knock his barbiton onto the floor.

"Jonathan!" cried his father. "What's the matter?"

"My stomach!" cried Jonathan, and then. "Aaaaah! Feels like I've swallowed shards of clay! Urrrrgh!"

"Great Neptune's beard," exclaimed Flavia's father.

"Oh dear!" Cartilia said. "Oh dear!"

Flavia's face had gone blank for a moment, but now there was a look of concern on it. "Jonathan!" she cried. "It must have been a bad oyster! Oh Jonathan! I'm so sorry I made you eat it!"

His ploy had worked. Her anger was forgotten.

"I forgive you." Jonathan smiled, then remembered he was supposed to be in agony. "Ahhhh!" He writhed again and curled up into a ball so they wouldn't see his expression. He had caught a glimpse of Lupus's narrowed eyes. One person, at least, had seen through his ruse.

Jonathan knew that if he looked at Lupus again he would burst out laughing. So he pressed his face into one of the cushions on the dining couch and bit it hard.

# SCROLL XVII

The next morning Jonathan and Lupus found Flavia in the dining room. She was sitting in her usual place on one of the dining couches, sipping her poculum and watching Hercules. It was a lovely morning: bright and clear and almost mild.

"Are you feeling better today, Jonathan?" asked Flavia after she had greeted the boys. She patted the dust sheet beside her and Jonathan and Lupus hopped up onto it.

"Yes, I'm much better," said Jonathan. The look of genuine concern on her face made him feel quite guilty. "Father gave me an infusion of camomile mixed with syrup of figs. He said it probably wasn't the oyster, just indigestion from eating while reclining."

"But everybody knows it's better for you to eat lying down. Anyway," Flavia lowered her voice, "I'm glad you had a stomach-ache when you did. I almost got myself locked up for the rest of the year, Saturnalia or no Saturnalia."

"Why?" asked Jonathan innocently.

"I was about to tell Cartilia where she could put her tam-bourine."

Lupus held up his wax tablet:

## WHERE IS NUBIA?

"Yes," said Jonathan. "Is she all right? Yesterday evening, she ran out of the room in the middle of a song."

Flavia frowned. "She's still in bed. She said she wasn't feeling well. Maybe it was something we ate." Then her eyes widened. "Maybe Cartilia is trying to poison us!" Flavia pressed her hand experimentally against her stomach and frowned. "Do I feel sick?"

"I don't think she's trying to poison us," said Jonathan. "You know, Flavia . . ."

"Yes?" Flavia turned her head to look at him. "What?"

"I don't think Cartilia is evil. I think she's quite nice. In fact . . ." his voice trailed off.

"What?" Flavia narrowed her eyes. "What in fact?"

Jonathan took a deep breath. "She reminds me a bit of you."

Flavia opened her mouth to reply, but at that moment Nubia came into the room.

Jonathan breathed a sigh of relief.

"I'll ignore Jonathan's last remark," said Flavia coolly. "Now that Nubia's here, let's review the facts. In my dream, Hercules told me I must complete twelve tasks. I believe the tasks are clues to solving a mystery that will save my father from Cartilia's evil clutches."

The four friends were still in the dining room, watching the wall painter work on the last wall. Now Flavia twisted to look at the wall behind them and gestured toward the fresco of Hercules wrestling a lion. "After we captured the lion," she said, "we learned that Cartilia was one of three daughters, and that the one nick-named Paula was a bit strange."

Flavia pointed to the next painting. It showed Hercules cutting snaky heads off a doglike creature.

"Then we visited the Wise Woman of Ostia near the hydra fountain. She directed us to Cartilia's house. So that was the second task completed. The third task of Hercules was to capture the

101

deer sacred to Diana. We found Diana, rather than the deer, but we discovered that Cartilia's nickname is Paula."

"And that her sister Diana is a bit strange, too," said Jonathan.

## I DON'T THINK SHE'S STRANGE

wrote Lupus.

Jonathan grinned.

Flavia gestured at the last scene painted on the wall behind them. "Hercules' fourth task was the boar," she continued. "At the Baths of Atalanta, near a boar mosaic, Nubia and I overheard a conversation and discovered a possible motive. Cartilia might be planning to marry my father and then kill him off to get her hands on his supposed wealth."

Jonathan folded his arms, "So far," he said, "all this is theory. And some of your informants were drunk as weasels."

"*In vino veritas,*" quoted Flavia. "In wine there is truth."

Lupus nodded his agreement and Flavia pointed to the central wall. "Hercules' fifth task led us to the stables, where we found out that Cartilia had been asking which baths Taurus the gladiator used!"

"I do have to admit that's strange," said Jonathan, unfolding his arms.

"And while you were hunting the Stymphalian bird—task number six—you discovered that Cartilia is a greedy old witch."

"According to her sister," said Jonathan.

"Meanwhile, at the Forum Baths, we discovered that Taurus the Cretan Bull—obviously our seventh task—was selling his bath scrapings. And that Cartilia bought not one but two bottles."

Jonathan shuddered. "And again I say, ewww."

"Task number eight," said Flavia, "led us to Diomedes the priest of Mithras. He gave us our most crucial piece of evidence. 'It was her fault,' he said. And he clearly meant the death of Cartilia's first husband, because he mentioned Caldus."

"That is a pretty serious accusation," said Jonathan. "Was he drunk?"

Flavia shook her head. "Sober as a Vestal."

Jonathan sighed.

"So we have four tasks left," said Flavia, opening her wax tablet and leaning back against the red wall. "The Amazon's belt, the Red Cattle, the Golden Apples, and Cerberus the Hound of Hades. Before we investigate them, I want to know what you think."

Lupus started writing on his wax tablet.

## SOMETHING NOT RIGHT
## ABOUT CARTILIA
## SHE IS NICE EVEN WHEN FLAVIA IS RUDE

"I'm not *that* rude to her," protested Flavia.

"Yes you are," said Jonathan. He ignored her glare. "I like Cartilia. I think she really loves your father, and the fact that she's being so nice to you is proof of that."

"That's your opinion," said Flavia briskly. "What about you, Nubia? You're good at sensing when people are hiding things."

Nubia was quiet for a moment. "Cartilia is being very nice to me. But when you were asking about her dead husband on first night, her face is pale. As if guilty."

Flavia nodded. "And there's something else we're forgetting," she said.

They all looked at her.

"The note. Diana gave Aristo a note asking him to meet her at the shrine."

Lupus wrote on his tablet:

## THAT'S NOT STRANGE
## DIANA LOVES ARISTO

"And yet the note was signed Cartilia. Doesn't it seem odd that Diana signed her note Cartilia?"

"Her name is Cartilia, too," said Jonathan.

"I know. But why sign it Cartilia instead of Diana?" Flavia lowered her voice. "I have a theory. What if Diana was only the messenger, even if she loves Aristo? Lupus says Aristo doesn't even like Diana. So what if the note was really from Cartilia? Cartilia Paula, I mean."

They stared at her.

"But Cartilia loves your father," said Jonathan.

"Does she?" Flavia thoughtfully sucked a strand of hair. "Lupus, could the woman at the shrine have been Cartilia?"

Lupus shrugged and then nodded. He wrote on his wax tablet.

## THEIR VOICES ARE VERY SIMILAR

"But why?" said Jonathan. "Why would Cartilia want to meet Aristo?"

"That's what I'm trying to discover," said Flavia. "Nubia. The woman in the woods. The one kissing Aristo. Is there any chance she could have been Cartilia?"

"Yes, there is any chance," said Nubia. "It could be any woman, if slim and not so tall."

For a moment they were all silent, watching Hercules spread fresh plaster on the last wall of the dining room.

Then Lupus held up his wax tablet apologetically:

## EVEN MIRIAM?

"Lupus!" cried Flavia and Jonathan at the same time.

"Don't be yelling at Lupus," said Nubia quietly. "Everybody knows Aristo is loving Miriam."

"It couldn't have been Miriam," said Jonathan. "She's been at my aunt's house since the morning after the betrothal ceremony. And Nubia saw Aristo kissing the woman the following afternoon."

"Besides," said Flavia, "Miriam loves my uncle and I'm sure she's faithful to him."

They all nodded.

Jonathan raised his hand. "Um, Flavia? Why don't we just ask Aristo who he was kissing?"

"We can't ask him," whispered Flavia. "What if Cartilia is using her love potion to enchant him, too!"

Nubia gasped. "Why?" she asked.

"So that he'll be under her spell and help her accomplish her evil scheme!"

# SCROLL XVIII

The Wise Woman sat in the weak winter sunshine and spun her gray wool. As Nubia's shadow fell across her lap the old woman squinted up at her. Nubia clapped her hands softly and let her knees bend.

"Ah, the lovely Nubia!" Lusca showed her single tooth in a smile. "Come, sit beside me. Shoo there!" She put the mass of soft wool on her lap and pushed the gray cat off the stool. The cat landed on the cold paving stones, blinked up at them with green eyes, then nonchalantly began to clean itself.

Nubia sat on the stool and extended a small papyrus parcel.

"Halva!" The papyrus crinkled as the old woman undid the folds. "Very tasty and easy on my gums. Thank you my dear."

The Wise Woman peered about. "Where's your bossy young mistress?"

"She is not my mistress," said Nubia quietly. "She set me free three months ago."

"Loyalty." The old woman nodded. "I like that. But I think she is still your mistress in many ways."

Nubia was silent. The gray cat rubbed itself against her leg and purred.

"Your friend is a truth seeker," said the old woman, "and she has a warm heart. But she has not yet learned that the truth can be dangerous. And sometimes painful. Also she tries to control people. This is never good. She must learn to trust the gods."

"I want to help her," said Nubia. "To help her find the truth."

"Then tell her this. Most of the evil in the world arises from two sources: greed and passion. She has been looking for actions motivated by greed. But in this particular case the troublemaker is Cupid, not Divitiae."

"Who is Divity Eye?"

"Not who. What." The old woman closed her eyes and sighed. "Though it should be a god. 'Divitiae' means wealth and only one deity has more power in the hearts of Romans: Cupid, the god of desire. Sometimes called Amor. Or Eros. Your friend Flavia should look to him."

"Thank you," said Nubia. "I think I understand. Thank you."

The old woman's eyes were still closed and her face turned up to the mild winter sun. In its light her skin was as translucent as parchment. The spindle lay among the wool in her lap.

Nubia reached down and stroked the purring cat. Presently she rose to go, then gasped as the old woman clutched her wrist.

"How old are you?" said the Wise Woman, opening her one good eye.

Nubia was too surprised to speak for a moment. "Eleven," she finally said. "I'm becoming twelve in summer."

The old woman nodded. "You also must beware of Cupid. You and your mistress. Neither of you are old enough yet. If you see him aim his bow, you must run. If by chance his arrow strikes, you must pluck it out, throw it far away, and take whatever cure you can find."

"Bossy young mistress," sighed Flavia. "Is that how people see me?" She had been hiding around the corner and had heard everything.

"Little bit," said Nubia. Then, seeing Flavia's expression, she quickly added, "Not so much."

"No." Flavia took Nubia's arm as they turned onto Mulberry

Street. "The old woman is right. I am bossy. But I'm glad I listened to you and let you question her your own way. I must try that some time."

"What?"

"Just sitting there and not saying anything."

"Silence is making people talk," said Nubia.

Flavia nodded. She could hear the faint sound of pipes and cymbals.

"I wonder if she's right about the motive," said Flavia presently. "Not greed, but passion. I need to think about that."

The music was louder and as they turned onto Orchard Street they converged with a funeral procession making for the Laurentum Gate. The girls moved up onto the pavement. They stood, their pallas wrapped around them, resting against the red brick wall between shuttered storefronts.

Weeping men and women led the procession and finally came the bier, a litter with the body of a girl whose profile looked very solemn and sad.

"Oh, Nubia!" whispered Flavia. "It's Bruta, the daughter of Brutus the pork butcher. She was to be married next month."

Marriage made Flavia think of Felix, as she did so many times each day, and she sighed. She closed her eyes and his face was there, as it always was. If you see Cupid aim his bow, the old woman had said. . . . No use running now. Cupid's arrow had struck her months ago and there seemed to be no cure. If anything, the sickness was getting worse. She could not even begin to think of marrying anyone else.

Flavia opened her eyes and shook her head.

"Come on," she said, taking Nubia's arm. "Hercules' ninth task was to get the belt of the Amazon. I've just remembered something. In the Temple of Rome and Augustus, Rome is shown as a beautiful Amazon resting her foot on the world. Let's go see if we can find our next clue there."

■■■

Nubia looked up into the vast space of the temple. Green marble columns rose up as high as the tallest palm trees in the oasis. High above her, a dove fluttered from the top of one column to the next.

Two priests, their heads draped with togas, were placing incense balls on braziers before the statue of Rome and Augustus. Pale gold beams of winter sunshine pierced the smoke that rose above them.

"There," whispered Flavia. "That's Augustus. He used to be an emperor but now he's a god."

"Augustus who is wearing five tunics because of the cold? He is now a god?"

"That's right. And the woman beside him is Rome as an Amazon."

"Rome is a girl with one breast not being covered?"

"Yes. That shows she's an Amazon. A brave female warrior. Sometimes Rome is depicted as an Amazon. And see? She has her foot on the world."

"That ball? That ball is being the world?" Nubia didn't understand. The sickly-sweet smell made her head spin and she reached for Flavia's hand.

"Yes," said Flavia. "And her foot shows that Rome has conquered it."

Nubia squinted through the incense smoke at the statue's lovely face. Then she turned to Flavia. "Rome-the-Amazon is looking familiar," she said.

"I was just thinking that." Flavia lowered her voice to a whisper, because one of the priests had turned to glare at her. "Now who does she remind me of?"

Suddenly Nubia knew.

She turned to Flavia. "The Amazon is looking just like Cartilia's sister, Diana."

# SCROLL XIX

Flavia took a deep breath and rapped the door knocker shaped like the club of Hercules. Nubia had been right. There was only one man-hating female warrior in the town. She knew the secret of the ninth clue—the clue of the Amazon's belt—had to lie with Cartilia's sister Diana.

Now Flavia's heart was pounding. What if Cartilia answered the door? Flavia knew she had been very rude to her the night before. She should never have revealed her true feelings like that. Now she must pretend to be sorry.

Perhaps nobody was home. That would almost be a relief.

The door swung open and a woman in a fine mesh hair net stood looking at them. It took Flavia a moment to recognize Cartilia's mother, Vibia. Without a wig, her natural hair was straight and gray.

"Oh. Hello, Flavia." Vibia's voice was flat. "Nubia. Please come in."

"Thank you," said Flavia, and took a deep breath. "Is Cartilia here. I mean Cartilia Paula?"

"No. My eldest daughter is at the baths." She led them through the atrium and into the study. There were no scrolls open on the desk and no pitcher of spiced wine.

"Do have a seat."

"Thank you." Flavia and Nubia sat in the same chairs they had sat in on their previous visit. This time Vibia did not offer them any refreshments. She sat stiffly in her chair and looked at the girls. Flavia thought she looked vulnerable without her elegant wig.

"Um . . . Does Cartilia Paula go to the Baths of Atalanta?" said Flavia, twisting the hem of her palla.

"Why do you suppose that?" replied Vibia, almost sharply. She shook her head. "No, both my daughters frequent the Baths of Minerva, a *respectable* establishment."

"Oh. Well, I wanted to see Cartilia because . . . I want to apologize to her. I was rude last night."

Vibia let out a breath. "I'm glad to hear it. You hurt my daughter deeply. She was weeping last night."

"What? Cartilia was crying?"

Vibia nodded. There were tears in her own eyes. "She has tried so hard to win your affection. Your approval."

"I made her cry?"

"Does it surprise you that a grown woman can cry?" Vibia's voice faltered. "You should have seen her when she got home, after your father said good-bye. She told me how angry you were about the tambourine. She thought you were just beginning to warm to her—" Vibia patted her hair and stood. "Oh dear. I shouldn't be telling you all this. But when she hurts, I hurt. She's still my little girl, you know."

"I'm sorry," said Flavia. She felt sick. "I really didn't know. . . . I'm sorry."

Vibia looked down at Flavia. "Paula desperately wants your approval, Flavia. She loves your father so very much. The day she met him—a few weeks ago—she came back here and I saw that for the first time in years the sparkle had returned to her eyes. Since then she's seemed to grow younger and happier. Until last week. I asked her what was wrong. At first she wouldn't say. Finally she said, 'His daughter hates me and I don't know why.'"

111

"I think," said Flavia, rising to her feet, "I think we have to go now."

"Wait." Vibia stepped forward and took Flavia's cold hands in her warm ones. "Thank you so much for coming to apologize. I can't tell you how much it will mean to Cartilia Paula. And how much it means to me."

"Yes. Well. We must go now. Come on, Nubia."

She was almost out of the front door when she felt Nubia catch her hand to stop her. Flavia turned, a rebuke on her lips, but she was silenced by Nubia's discovery: several cloaks hanging in the vestibule.

"That is a very nice cloak," Nubia said, pointing toward one in particular. "Is it Diana's?"

Vibia glanced at the cloaks hanging by the door. "What? The gray one with the hood?"

Nubia nodded.

"No," said Vibia with a smile. "That cloak belongs to me. Isn't it lovely? It's made of special wool from the goat's stomach and it's very warm. It was a gift to me from my husband."

# SCROLL XX

"Behold, Flavia! Mushrooms!" Nubia bent and lifted the basket from the front porch. A red ribbon was tied around the basket's handle and a papyrus label attached to it.

"Oh, Pollux," said Flavia. "They're from *her*. Now I really do feel bad."

Nubia looked at the papyrus label as Flavia read it out loud:

## MUSHROOMS WILL MAKE YOU
## A GOOD SATURNALIA
## THEY ARE STUFFED BY MY OWN HAND
## WITH LOVE
## FROM PAULA

"They look tasty," said Nubia.

"Pater's not here tonight," said Flavia. "He's dining at Cartilia's. But Jonathan and Aristo like mushrooms. Why don't we invite the boys and Doctor Mordecai around? Our storeroom is getting bare. They can bring the meat."

"Any luck with task number ten at the Red Cow Dairy?" asked Flavia.

Jonathan shook his head but Lupus nodded.

"Oh yes," said Jonathan with a grin. "Lupus won at dice."

"How much?" asked Flavia, arranging the stuffed mushrooms on a platter.

Lupus emptied a papyrus cone of almonds onto the wooden cutting board.

"*Euge!*" said Nubia. "I can prepare almond dates for dessert."

"Any luck finding clues about Cartilia?"

"No," said Jonathan. "But did you know there's a new tavern up by the river called the Atlas Tavern?"

"And . . . ?" Flavia added some dried parsley to garnish the platter of mushrooms.

"Well. When Hercules performed his eleventh task, to find the golden apples, didn't he get some help from Atlas?"

"Yes," said Flavia. "He held the world on his shoulders while Atlas went to get the apples from the garden of the Hesperides."

"So shouldn't we try the Atlas Tavern? We could go now!"

Lupus shook his dice box and nodded enthusiastically.

"No," sighed Flavia. "I'm thinking of calling off the whole investigation. We talked to Cartilia's mother today. It seems Cartilia really does love my father. Oh, and apparently her mother is Aristo's secret lover."

"What?"

"I don't know, Jonathan!" Flavia turned to look at him. "I'm so depressed. Brutus's daughter died and I made Cartilia cry and everything's so confusing. Let's just have a nice feast tonight and play some music and forget about our woes. Can you all come?"

Jonathan nodded. "Lupus and I can come but Father said he wouldn't be home till late. He has lots of sick patients at the moment."

"Can you bring some meat?"

Jonathan nodded again. "One of Father's patients paid him with a leg of wild boar. Father doesn't really like pork, so we'll bring that."

Suddenly there was a clatter from the dining room, then a thud. "What was that?" cried Jonathan.

Nipur skittered out of the kitchen and Scuto limped after him. The four friends followed them through the garden.

"In here!" Caudex the door slave was bending over a body on the floor of the triclinium.

It was Hercules the wall painter.

"Dear Lord, not another one." Mordecai straightened from the dining couch upon which they had laid Hercules. "I'm afraid he's got the fever, too. This is the sixth or seventh case this afternoon. He won't be going anywhere for at least two days. We need to get him home. Do any of you know where he lives?"

There was a pause. Lupus looked up from examining Hercules' paintbrush. Everyone was looking at him.

Lupus shrugged.

"We only know his name," said Flavia, then added, "Hercules."

"I know where he lives," said Caudex, scratching his armpit. "I can carry him."

"But who's going to finish painting the wall?" cried Flavia.

As they carried the wall painter out of the room, Lupus looked down at the paintbrush in his hand. And smiled.

Jonathan took a mushroom from the platter and nodded at Scuto. "He seems better now."

It was late afternoon and they had all gathered in Flavia's triclinium for dinner.

"Yes," said Flavia. "He was resting earlier but Nubia and I took him for a short walk in the woods about an hour ago."

"See anybody 'very kissing'?" grinned Jonathan. Then he clapped his hand over his mouth and looked at Aristo.

Flavia glanced at Aristo, too, but he was staring wide-eyed at the wall behind her.

Flavia twisted to look over her shoulder.

Somehow, the fresco had been completed and the sketches of the last two tasks expertly filled in with color. In the eleventh labour Hercules strained to hold the sky on his lion-covered shoulders while Atlas stood before him with three golden apples. In the final scene Hercules led a three-headed dog toward a man cowering in a huge jar.

"Hey!" said Jonathan, his mouth full. "Those two Herculeses look a bit like you, Flavia! Apart from the beard and muscles, of course."

"Very kissing?" said Aristo suddenly. "What do you mean by that?"

Flavia ignored him. "It is me!" she cried. "But we took Hercules the wall painter home! How did he manage to finish. . . ." She stopped and slowly turned her head to look at Lupus.

Lupus was staring at the ceiling, whistling a little tune.

"Aha!" cried Jonathan, holding up Lupus's right hand. "The proof! Paint on his fingers!"

"Lupus, did you finish those paintings?"said Flavia.

Lupus nodded and started writing on his tablet.

"They are wonderful," said Nubia. "Almost as good as wall painter."

Lupus held up his wax tablet:

# I HAD TO FINISH IT
# PLASTER DRIES FAST

"He's right," said Aristo, leaning forward to take a mushroom. "If you don't finish painting a fresco before the plaster dries you have to redo the whole wall. Or leave it unfinished."

"Well, I like them," said Jonathan, popping another mushroom into his mouth. "I think a beard suits Flavia."

"Who is man hiding in big jar?" asked Nubia.

"King Eurystheus," said Flavia. "He's the person Hercules had to serve for eight years while he did the tasks."

"He is looking a bit like your pater," said Nubia.

"Great Neptune's beard! Lupus! You've made him look like Pater!"

Lupus grinned and nodded.

"These mushrooms taste a bit odd." Aristo frowned.

Jonathan nodded. "Did you make them, Flavia?"

"No." Flavia turned away from the fresco. "They're from Cartilia." She reached for one. "Her note said she stuffed them herself."

"But what is the stuffing?" said Jonathan. "It's something brown. . . ."

"Olive paste?" suggested Aristo.

"Or thick fish sauce?" said Jonathan, chewing thoughtfully.

Suddenly Flavia's blood seemed to go cold.

"STOP!" she cried. "Don't eat them! They're poisoned!"

# SCROLL XXI

"What?" everyone cried. "Poisoned?"

"Yes!" said Flavia. "The mushrooms are poisoned! Cartilia is trying to kill us off because we're getting too close to the truth! She chose the one afternoon when Pater was out to murder us! I was right about her after all."

"What are you talking about?" said Aristo, sniffing a mushroom. "This doesn't smell very nice but I don't think it's poison. It smells like oil, and cumin perhaps?" He paused and sniffed again. "Cumin smells like sweat. . . ."

"Great Juno's peacock!" cried Flavia. "It's the love potion!"

"Love potion?" Aristo frowned.

Jonathan looked green. "You don't mean?"

"Yes," Flavia nodded grimly. "You've been eating mushrooms stuffed with gladiator scrapings!"

"Argghhh!" cried Jonathan. "Love mushrooms! I'd rather be poisoned!"

"By Apollo!" cried Aristo suddenly. "I'm going to murder her!" He slid awkwardly off the couch, jostling the table and causing the plate of mushrooms to clatter to the floor. The damp note had stuck to the bottom of the platter and now it lay on the floor, still attached to its red ribbon.

Aristo bent, picked up the papyrus and read it. Breathing hard, he looked at the dogs gobbling up the love mushrooms at his feet. Then he crumpled up the note and threw it to the ground.

"I swear I'm going to murder her!" he repeated, and rushed out of the room.

Flavia Gemina sat up straight on her banqueting couch and turned to Lupus.

"Follow him!" she hissed. "And don't let him see you."

Eyes bright, Lupus nodded, then jumped down from the couch and slipped out of the room.

Flavia looked round at the others. "Whoever Aristo goes to is the one behind all this," she said. "If Lupus doesn't lose him, we might finally solve this mystery."

Lupus followed Aristo through the dusk as silently as a shadow. Once he lost him in a crowd of revelers but by then he suspected where Aristo was going, so he took a short cut. He was already hiding behind the column of a neighbor's porch when Aristo banged on the door with the club door knocker.

Lupus listened with all his might, shutting out the sound of the wind in the trees and the singing from the Peacock Tavern.

He heard Aristo's voice, low and angry, then a woman's voice. The wind died for a moment and he faintly heard the woman call out, "Mater, may I borrow your cloak?"

Lupus took a breath and slipped closer to the porch of the nearest neighbor. The twilight around him was a vibrant blue. Nubia called it "hour of blue."

He listened and suddenly heard the crunch of boots on the paving stone and Aristo's voice almost in his ear. They were just the other side of the column!

"It was you who sent those mushrooms, wasn't it? You stuffed them with your disgusting potion. Did you really think that would work?"

"No, Aristo . . . it wasn't me. Don't look at me like that!"

119

"Then take that ridiculous wig off."

"But you don't like my short hair."

"I don't like that wig either. And don't try to change the subject. You sent those mushrooms. You pretended they were from your sister. Admit it!"

"All right. But I'm only telling you because I love you, Aristo, I don't want anything to come between us."

"Us? There is no 'us' . . . I don't love you. Dear gods, I don't even like you."

"But last week. In the woods. Didn't that mean anything to you? The way you held me, kissed me . . . You told me you loved me then. . . ."

Lupus heard Aristo groan. "Did I say I loved you? I was beside myself. Some god must have possessed me."

"It wasn't a god. It was her, wasn't it? You were thinking of her." Her voice was quiet, almost calm. "You called me something. What was it? Melania? Is that her name?"

"Diana, please. I'm sorry, but I don't love you."

"No. You love her. Is that it, Aristo? You love Melania and she won't have you? I'm right, aren't I?" There was a note of wonder in her voice. "So you closed your eyes and imagined I was her?"

There was a pause.

"Something like that."

"You vile crawling thing." Diana's voice was quiet. "If she causes you half as much pain as you've caused me then I'll be glad."

"Be glad," Aristo said miserably.

Flavia's eyes grew wider and wider as Lupus wrote out the conversation he had just overheard. The four friends sat on the central dining couch near a brazier full of glowing coals. Outside in the garden, night had fallen.

"Diana!" breathed Flavia, as she watched Lupus write. "Diana was the one Aristo was kissing!"

Lupus nodded.

"So she borrowed her mother's cloak? The one with the hood?"

Lupus nodded again and added three words to his tablet.

## AND HER WIG

"I'm an idiot!" said Flavia pulling a blanket tighter around her shoulders. "I should have realized it was Diana. Look at this label, the one that came with the mushrooms. The handwriting is the same as the note Diana gave to Aristo. I don't know why I ever thought it was Cartilia."

"You haven't been thinking very clearly," said Jonathan.

"I know," sighed Flavia. "And I'm still confused."

"Me, too," said Jonathan, handing back the papyrus. "I understand the bit about Diana loving Aristo. But why did Diana sign the label Paula?"

"Maybe because Aristo wouldn't have touched the mushrooms if he knew they were from Diana," said Flavia.

"Ugh!" Jonathan shuddered. "I can't believe I ate three of those things. I hope I don't fall in love with Diana!"

## SHE'S NOT THAT BAD

wrote Lupus.

"Oooh!" said Jonathan. "Lupus loves Diana! Did you eat some tasty love mushrooms, Lupus? Ha!" Jonathan laughed as Lupus wrestled him to the couch. Nipur and Tigris barked with excitement.

"Be careful, you two!" cried Flavia. "You'll knock over the brazier and set the whole house on fire!"

When the boys had calmed down Nubia said, "I think Diana is being jealous of Cartilia. In my clan I was having a friend who always strives with her sister."

"Nubia, you may be right," said Flavia. "Diana hasn't even been married once and her sister is about to marry for a second time.

That's probably why she said Cartilia was a greedy old witch. She meant greedy for husbands, not money." Suddenly she gasped. "Oh no!"

"What?" said Jonathan.

"I've just had a terrible thought. What if Diana didn't just sign Cartilia's name on notes. What if she actually pretended to be Cartilia?"

"But Diana has short hair."

"Yes," said Flavia. "And her mother has a wig! I'll bet Diana's been telling everyone she's Paula: Fimus at the stables, Oleosus at the baths. . . ."

Flavia looked at her friends. "We haven't got much time to find the truth. Tomorrow is the last day of the Saturnalia. We have two labors left: the Golden Apples and Cerberus the Hound of Hades. Jonathan, you and Lupus check out the Atlas Tavern, the one you were telling me about. Find out whether Diana could have been impersonating her sister. And find out anything you can about Cartilia's dead husband. That's the one thing I still don't understand. Why she acts so strange whenever I mention him."

"All right," said Jonathan. "How about you and Nubia? Are you going to pay a visit to the underworld?"

Nubia made the sign against evil but Flavia nodded slowly.

"In a way," she said. "Yes, in a way we are."

# SCROLL XXII

Flavia took Nubia's hand as they gazed down at the tomb of Avita Procula. In the gray light of an overcast morning the fresco of the little girl and her dog looked flat and dull.

Although she had never met the girl whose ashes lay there, Flavia felt she was looking at a friend's grave.

"Coming here makes me think of the first mystery we solved together. Do you remember, Nubia?"

Nubia nodded, not taking her eyes from the fresco of the little girl lying on her death couch. Scuto and Nipur had watered their favorite trees and came up to sniff the tomb.

"Can you believe it was only six months ago?" said Flavia. "It seems like so much longer."

"Her tomb is making me think of wild dogs," said Nubia.

"And of the three-headed *thing*. . . ." Flavia shivered. "That's why we're here. The final task of Hercules was to bring Cerberus back from the land of the dead. This is the only place I could think of which is a bit like the underworld."

"I hope we do not meet any wild dogs," said Nubia.

"Me too." Flavia ruffled Scuto's head and looked around. "We've been here nearly half an hour. There's nobody here. I don't understand. The clues of Hercules haven't failed us yet."

Nubia touched her arm. "Listen. Do you hear that noise?"

Flavia listened, then nodded.

"Over there," said Nubia suddenly, pointing toward some umbrella pines. "There is someone sitting at bottom of tree."

"You're right. It's a young hunter . . . no! It's Diana, and . . . and she's crying!"

"I guess this is the one," said Jonathan, stopping in front of the tavern and peering up at the crude fresco over the wide doorway. "Does that look like Atlas holding up the sky?"

## I COULD PAINT A BETTER ATLAS

wrote Lupus.

"You already did. At Flavia's." Jonathan grinned and then shook his head. "If Father knew I was going into a tavern . . ." He went up the three steps, then moved to the bar and rested his forearms on the marble counter. Its smooth, cream-colored surface was inlaid with a pattern of green and pink squares. Lupus leaned on the counter beside him.

"Good morning, boys!" said the innkeeper. "What can I get you?"

"Two cups of hot spiced wine," said Jonathan, with as much confidence as he could muster. "Well-watered please."

"Certainly. Would you like extra pepper?"

Jonathan nodded.

The innkeeper dipped his ladle into a hole in the bar. Jonathan leaned over and looked in. The wine jar was actually sunk into the bar. Clever. The man filled two ceramic beakers half full of a wine so dark it was almost black, then topped up the mixture with hot water from a silver urn. Finally he sprinkled some pepper on top.

"There you are."

"How much?"

"Three sestercii."

Jonathan fished in his coin pouch for a denarius. He put the silver coin on the counter and sipped the wine.

The innkeeper took the denarius and slid a copper sestercius back across the marble surface. "Tasty?"

"Very." Jonathan took a breath and before the innkeeper could turn away he said, "My friend Cartilia Poplicola hasn't been in today, has she?" It was a feeble question but Flavia had told them to try anything.

"No," said the innkeeper, and jerked his thumb over his shoulder. "But her husband's here."

"Wh-ghak!" Jonathan nearly choked on his wine and Lupus coughed so hard he had to be patted on the back.

"Sorry," said the innkeeper. "Too much pepper?"

"Cartilia's *husband*? Her *dead* husband?"

The innkeeper chuckled. "Caldus is a bit hungover but I wouldn't call him dead. That's him right over there in the court-yard. Talking to his friends. He arrived from Rome last night. He's the big fellow in the brown cloak."

# SCROLL XXIII

"Hello, Diana." Flavia sat cross-legged on the damp pine needles in front of the weeping girl. Nubia sat gracefully beside her. Scuto and Nipur greeted the huntress with cold noses and wagging tails.

Diana looked up at them with swollen eyes, then dropped her head. "Go away."

Flavia and Nubia exchanged glances.

Presently Diana lifted her head again. "Why aren't you going away?"

"We want to comfort you," lied Flavia.

"So he's told you? He's told you all about poor lovesick Diana?"

"No," said Flavia. "Aristo hasn't said anything. We guessed."

"Oh." Diana hugged her legs and pressed her forehead on her knees for a moment. She was wearing Vibia's gray, hooded cape over her short red tunic.

"You're so lucky," Diana whispered at last. "You can be with him every day."

Flavia opened her mouth to say something, then remembered what Nubia had taught her and closed it again.

"I remember the first time I saw him," whispered Diana. "Two years ago. I thought he was a god come down from Olympus. He was walking out of the woods with Lysander. He'd caught a deer.

A beautiful dead doe. I longed to be that creature, draped over his shoulders."

Diana's head was still down and her voice was muffled. "That was when I decided to become a hunter. And about a year ago I finally met him. Sometimes we went hunting together, with Lysander. Then Aristo went away for the summer and when he came back he seemed distant. He barely looked at me."

Diana shivered and pulled her cloak tighter around her.

"Last month I found him hunting in the woods alone. I went up to him and told him how I felt. It was the bravest thing I've ever done. And he . . . he looked at me as if I was demented. He told me he could never love me."

In the tree above them, a bird trilled its sweet song.

"That was when I cut off my hair and dedicated it to Diana. I vowed I would never marry, that I'd be a virgin forever. Aristo didn't like my short hair. And he didn't like me calling myself Diana. But I didn't care. I felt new and strong. At first. Then, when the gladiator arrived and they said he was selling love potion, I couldn't resist. I bought a jar and put it in the quail pie."

"Can I just ask . . ." said Flavia. "You know you're supposed to put some of your bodily fluids in it . . ."

Diana looked up at them with liquid eyes. "Tears," she whispered. "I added my tears."

Flavia breathed a sigh of relief and waited.

"Last week I was hunting in the grove. It was afternoon. The first day of the Saturnalia. I heard a noise. It was him. Weeping. I thought that perhaps the potion had worked. . . . So I went to him, took his face in my hands. He let me kiss away his tears and then he was kissing me back. And then . . . and then." She hugged her knees tightly.

"But later he grew distant again. So I bought more potion. But yesterday he told me he didn't love me and I realized it had never been the potion. I was a fool. And now my sister is going to be married for the second time. It's not fair. I hate her! And I hate Melania, whoever she is. But most of all I hate Aristo!"

Scuto sensed Diana's distress and put a comforting paw on her arm. At this, she burst into tears.

"And I wish . . ." sobbed Diana. "I wish I were dead!"

The courtyard of the Atlas Tavern was filled with the pearly light of a cloudy day and the smell of sizzling sausage. There was an ivy-covered trellis against one wall, a small bubbling fountain, and a single wooden table with long benches on either side. Four men sat at this table, and although they were not wearing togas, Lupus could see immediately that they were highborn.

"How are we going to approach him?" whispered Jonathan. "We can't just march up to him and say, 'Hello, why aren't you dead?'"

Lupus shrugged.

Then he grinned as he heard a sound he recognized. The rattle of dice in a wooden box.

He knew exactly how to break the ice.

Flavia ran to her front door, slid back the bolt, and threw it open.

She and Jonathan stood face to face.

"You'll never believe what we found out!" they both cried at the same time. And laughed.

"You first," said Jonathan. He and Lupus followed Flavia through the atrium into the study. Nubia was already there, warming her hands over the coal-filled brazier. It was still early in the afternoon but the red sun had already slipped behind the city wall and the inner garden was in cold shadow.

"We discovered," said Flavia, "that Diana has been in love with Aristo for nearly two years. She's angry at him because he got her hopes up last week only to dash them again. Also, she's furious that her sister is engaged for the second time."

wrote Lupus.

"I'd feel sorry for her, too, if she hadn't gone around town pretending to be Cartilia."

"She admitted it?" said Jonathan.

Flavia nodded. "She said she'd put on her mother's wig and cloak and kept her head down. She told Oleosus the bath slave that her name was Paula. And she's the one who asked Fimus where Taurus the gladiator bathed."

Jonathan nodded. "Because she didn't want anyone to know Diana the virgin huntress was out buying love potion!"

Flavia stared at the glowing embers and nodded. "I hate to admit it, but it looks as if I was wrong about Cartilia. She's innocent. Her husband must have died of natural causes."

"No," said Jonathan, folding his arms. "He didn't. That's our news."

Flavia looked at him, wide-eyed. "He was murdered? You have proof?"

"He wasn't murdered and he didn't die of natural causes," said Jonathan. "In fact he's not dead at all. He's alive and well and staying at the Atlas Tavern."

Flavia opened her mouth but no sound came out. Finally she managed a squeaky, "What?"

"He's down from Rome. Staying at the Atlas Tavern. We gamed with him. We won two dozen walnuts and we learned that he divorced Cartilia."

Flavia gasped. "He divorced her?"

Jonathan nodded.

"But that's wonderful!"

"I know," said Jonathan. "Now your father can marry her and he'll be happy and you'll have a mother again."

"Cartilia will never be my mother," said Flavia fiercely. "She's the one trying to marry me off and keep me indoors. It's wonderful because it means she lied to Pater. Now I'll be able to get rid of her and keep things just the way they are!"

Flavia had no time to waste. She put her plan into action immediately. Lupus delivered her carefully worded message and returned before anybody missed him, just as they were all gathering for the last dinner of the Saturnalia.

Flavia was so nervous she could hardly eat her ostrich stew. When the knock came at the front door her heart started pounding, and her hands were shaking, so she put her spoon down.

"Man here to see you, master."

"Caudex!" cried Captain Geminus, climbing off the couch. "What are you doing here? It's the last day of the holiday! You should be down at the tavern enjoying yourself."

"Feeling a little tired, master. Thought I'd come home, have a rest."

"Well, show this fellow in and then go and have your rest. . . . Who did you say he was?"

"Name's Caldus. He says he got your message."

Flavia glanced up at Cartilia. And almost burst out laughing at the look of surprise on the woman's face. Flavia kept her head down and bit her lip.

"Caldus?" said Flavia's father. "I don't know anyone named Caldus."

"Says he got a message from you."

"Well, I suppose you'd better show him in."

"Marcus, no. Send him away." Cartilia was trying to get off the couch but a table blocked her descent.

"Sweetheart! What's the matter?" Flavia's father pushed the table aside and lifted her down.

"I have to go! I can't stay here!" Cartilia turned and started for the doorway, then stopped as a figure in a brown cloak blocked her

130

way. He was a red-faced man, as tall as Flavia's father but broader.

"Cartilia!" His eyes widened as he looked down at her. "Cartilia, is this some kind of joke?"

"Postumus," she stammered. "Postumus, what are you doing here?"

"I got a message." He frowned around at them all. "Who are these people?"

"I'm Marcus Flavius Geminus, sea captain. This is my home. May I ask the nature of your business with Cartilia?" Flavia's father stood behind Cartilia with his hands protectively on her shoulders.

"Oh, so that's it!" Caldus snorted. "Trying to make me jealous, Cartilia? Or do you just want to rub my nose in it?"

"Cartilia, who is this man?"

Flavia felt almost sorry for Cartilia as she said, "Marcus, it's my husband. I'm sorry. I was going to tell you. . . ."

"Your husband? But you said he was dead!"

Caldus gave a bark of laughter. "What? Tried to kill me off, did you? Not a bad idea. Far better to be a grieving widow than a divorced woman."

"You're divorced?" Marcus looked down at Cartilia. "Why didn't you tell me?'

Cartilia was silent, so Caldus answered.

"Because if she told you she was divorced she'd have to tell you the reason why! Looks like the joke's on you, Cartilia. Why don't you tell Captain Square-jaw here why I divorced you? Go on!"

"No!" Cartilia covered her face with her hands.

Caldus folded his muscular arms and looked down at her, then up at Flavia's father. "I divorced her," he said, "because she was incapable of giving me children. And because she was too damned independent!"

131

# SCROLL XXIV

Flavia lay awake for a long time, going over the events of the evening.

After Caldus had left, her father and Cartilia had gone into the study.

In the dining room, while eating their dessert, they heard Flavia's father say, "How can I marry you now? You've broken our trust!"

A short time later the front door had closed and her father had gone heavily upstairs to his room.

The marriage was off. Cartilia was out of their lives. Flavia's plan had worked perfectly. She had won, but for some reason the victory seemed flat.

She rolled over on her side and gazed at her Felix doll, its face barely visible in the dim light of a night lamp.

"I did the right thing, didn't I?" she asked him.

The doll did not reply.

"It was my task," she whispered. "Pater wants descendants and Cartilia wouldn't have been able to give him children. That must be why the gods wanted me to get rid of her."

The Felix doll gazed back at her impassively.

"She lied to him! She broke his trust!"

In the flickering light the doll's tiny black eyes were steady.

"Don't look at me like that," said Flavia. "I know I did the right thing. Now things will be back to normal. Just the way they were."

The next morning, it did seem as if things were back to normal. The Saturnalia was over. Alma made breakfast and Caudex unwrapped the ivy from the columns. Captain Geminus quietly made his offering at the lararium and went out early.

They resumed their lessons and after the boys went home Flavia and Nubia took the dogs for a walk among the tombs.

It was noon and the sun was shining bravely.

As they approached a clearing, the dogs froze and Scuto growled.

"Behold!" breathed Nubia. "The camelopard."

"Great Neptune's beard," gasped Flavia.

The camelopard stood in the pale sunshine. It had a body like a horse and a head like a camel, and its neck was immensely long. It was browsing among the branches of an acacia tree.

"Shhh, Scuto! Quiet!" commanded Flavia. "Oh, Nubia, he's beautiful. Look at the pattern on his skin, and his long eyelashes. And his tongue is blue!"

They watched the camelopard until it moved slowly off into the woods.

The dogs looked up at the girls and Scuto gave a whining gulp.

"Good boy, Scuto!" said Flavia. "You didn't chase it away." She turned to Nubia. "One of us should go and tell Mnason. Shall I?"

"I will seek him," said Nubia. "Then I can greet Monobaz. I will run now swifter than the wind, before some hunters kill the giraffe."

"What did you call it?"

"Giraffe. That is what we are calling him in my country."

"I'll take the dogs back home then," said Flavia and laughed as Nubia sprinted for the Fountain Gate.

Flavia followed the dogs slowly back. The day was almost warm.

Birds were singing. The sky was blue. She wouldn't have to battle with a stepmother and there would be no more talk of marrying. Not yet.

And maybe one day—when she was sixteen and miraculously beautiful—Felix would carry her over the threshold in his arms. She didn't know how it might happen, but at least it was a possibility again.

Flavia felt a huge surge of euphoria as she pushed open the back door. Life was wonderful. It held the intoxicating promise of anything and everything.

Scuto and Nipur went straight to the kitchen and their water bowls. Flavia followed and hung their leads on the peg as they lapped thirstily.

"Pater?" she called happily. "We saw the camelopard! Pater? Alma?"

Flavia bounced into the study, then stopped short. "Pater, what's wrong?"

Her father was sitting at his desk with his head in his hands.

Flavia felt a cold sinking sensation, right down to her toes. "Pater," she said in a horrified whisper. "Are you crying?"

He lifted his head and looked at her. His eyes were red and his cheeks wet.

"Oh, Pater! Don't cry. Please don't cry." Flavia ran to him and threw her arms around his neck.

"No!" He pushed her away. "I just want to be alone. Please."

"Shall I make you some mint tea? Would that cheer you up?"

"I don't want to see you right now, Flavia. Please go away."

"What?"

"You sent that message, didn't you?" he said, then shook his head. "It doesn't matter. Just go away."

"But Pater. . . ." Her throat hurt and tears pricked her own eyes.

"GO AWAY!"

He rested his head on his arms and his shoulders shook.

Flavia looked down at him for a moment. Then she turned and ran out of the room.

"Oh, hello Flavia," said Jonathan, standing in the open doorway. "You just missed him."

Tigris greeted Flavia with a wag of his tail and began sniffing her feet with great interest.

"What?" said Flavia, blinking back tears.

"You just missed him."

"Who?"

"Felix. He left a few minutes ago."

"What?" gasped Flavia. "My Felix?"

Jonathan nodded. "He stopped by to pick up some more elixir."

"Some more what?"

"Elixir. For his wife."

Flavia stared at Jonathan. Nipur had moved on from sniffing her feet to sniffing the gutter.

"You remember his wife Polla wasn't well?"

"What do you mean, 'Polla wasn't well?' She was barking mad."

"Father says she was just depressed. He sent her some tonic last September and apparently it had an amazing effect. Felix was travelling back from Rome to Surrentum today, so he stopped by to pick up some more and discuss the dose with Father."

"He was here in your house? Just now?" Flavia felt as if someone had kicked her in the stomach.

Jonathan nodded. "Don't you want to come in?"

"And you saw him?"

"Not for very long."

"Did he . . ." Flavia felt sick. "Did he mention me?"

"He said we must all come and stay with them again next summer."

"He . . . What were his exact words?"

"Um . . . 'You must all come and stay with us again next summer.' Those were his exact words."

"So he didn't mention me at all? Not even to ask how I was?"

"Tigris! Come here! Get away from that!" Jonathan focused on Flavia again. "Sorry, Flavia. I think Felix was in a rush to get back. He was traveling light, on horseback with just two of his men."

Flavia looked at Jonathan. His face seemed strange. Everything seemed strange. Why was she standing here in front of his open door on the bright pavement? Something was moaning. Just the wind. When had the wind started to blow?

Jonathan's face was sympathetic. "Flavia," he said gently. "Come in and have some mint tea. It will—TIGRIS! I said get away from that! BAD DOG! Come here at once!"

"Excuse me," said Flavia. "I'm just . . ."

She turned toward her house, then remembered her weeping father and turned back to Jonathan. But he was bending over Tigris, struggling to drag the big puppy back into the house.

Flavia turned away and walked slowly past her front door, the blue one with the Castor and Pollux knocker. She walked past the brown door with its lion's head door knocker, past the yellow door and the faded green one. Her step quickened. Faster and faster, until she was running. If she hurried she might just catch him.

She thought she heard Jonathan calling her but she kept her head down and ran. Past the green fountain. Out through the Fountain Gate. And down the tomb-lined road in the direction of Surrentum.

# SCROLL XXV

"Flavia! Flavia, where are you?"

Nubia shut the back door and let the bolt fall. She bent to greet the wagging dogs, then stood and looked around.

"Flavia!" she called again. "I am just now helping Mnason to catch the camelopard."

No reply. The house was silent. Only the sound of the wind moaning in the eves.

"Alma? Caudex?" Nubia frowned. "Captain Geminus?"

She went along the columned peristyle and through the corridor to the atrium. The door to Alma's cubicle was slightly ajar.

"Alma?"

As Nubia scratched on the door, it swung open.

Alma lay on the bed, a cloth draped across her forehead. She groaned and turned her head.

"Oh, Nubia," she murmured. "Not feeling too well. Bit hot. And my ears are buzzing. Just having a little rest. Caudex resting, too. Will you ask Doctor Mordecai . . . Will you ask . . . Will you . . . ?"

Doctor Mordecai shook his turbaned head. "This is bad," he said to Nubia. "Very bad. Lupus came down with a fever around noon and I've just put Jonathan to bed, too. And now both Alma and Caudex. How do you feel?" He pressed his hand to her forehead.

"I am fine," said Nubia.

"And Flavia?" said Doctor Mordecai. "How is she?"

"I don't know. She is not here. I think she is out with her father."

Mordecai shook his head again. "If I get many more cases it will be an epidemic. And I may not be able to attend everyone. Nubia?"

"Yes?"

"Can you make sure Alma and Caudex have plenty to drink? And keep them warm? They may want to kick off the covers, but they need to sweat out the fever. I'll have to treat them later. Do you understand?"

"Yes, Doctor Mordecai."

"Can you make up a pot of broth? Chicken preferably. But anything clear and with some meat in it."

"Yes, Doctor Mordecai."

"You're a good girl," said Mordecai. "Bless you." He rested his hand lightly on her head and she felt a sort of tingly warmth pass through her.

Nubia hoped it was not the fever.

Flavia waited for him under an acacia tree. Above her, the wind was moaning. In the space of an hour the temperature had plunged. The sun—exhausted from trying to warm the world on one of his weakest days—was sinking toward the red horizon.

Flavia looked up at the rattling leaves. She wore only her tunic and she knew she should feel cold. But for some reason she felt curiously warm.

Presently her patience was rewarded. She heard him before she saw him. A strange buzzy pulsing tune filled her ears. It was unlike any she had ever heard. At last he came into view, gliding down the road between the tombs. He was riding a lion and he wore a garland of grape leaves. Strange creatures danced behind him. Mythical beasts who were partly man and partly goat. The satyrs played double flutes and shook tambourines. Behind them came a huge dog with three nodding heads: one white, one black, one red.

Flavia didn't care about the satyrs. She didn't care about Cerberus. She only cared about him. She struggled to her feet and called his name.

Felix turned his head and looked at her. Then he climbed down from the lion. Monobaz rolled at his feet, like Scuto when he wanted his stomach scratched. Felix took out a sharp knife, bent over, and with one swift motion he cut the lion open.

"No!" Flavia cried. "Not Monobaz!"

But it was too late. Felix smiled and walked toward her, holding the empty lion skin in his hands.

"It's all right," said Monobaz's head. "I don't mind."

Felix put the lion's head on her, as if it were a hat, then he wrapped the empty paws around her shoulders. The fur was soft and warm. She looked up into his handsome face and he smiled down at her with his dangerous dark eyes. She didn't know if he was a man or a god.

"Felix?" she whispered.

He nodded and placed a heavy shield gently on her head. Then he took first her right hand and then her left hand, lifting them up so that they supported the shield on either side.

Then he backed away.

"Felix!" she called after him. "Come back! I love you!"

But now he was moving off down the road again, playing his lyre, his head back and his eyes closed. Behind him danced a crowd of people.

Jonathan and Miriam came first, and Mordecai too. Nubia danced behind them, playing her flute. Then came Lupus, banging his goatskin drum with a sponge stick. Aristo followed, and then Diana, clutching the hem of his red cloak. Caudex and Alma skipped hand in hand. Pulchra was there, with her little sisters and her slave girl Leda.

Then came Avita and her father Avitus. There was Captain Alga,

139

old Pliny and young Pliny. And Phrixus. Vulcan rode his donkey. Rectina and Tascius and their nine daughters danced behind.

"No," cried Flavia. "You should have eleven now."

The shield on her head was getting heavier and heavier.

"Why is it so heavy?" she asked Sisyphus.

"My dear," he said, "it's because you're carrying the weight of the world." And he jumped lightly up to join the others on the shield.

"Do you want me up there, too?" asked the Emperor Titus.

"No," said Flavia. "I can't hold you all."

But he climbed up anyway.

"No, it's too heavy for me," sobbed Flavia. "I can't hold it. Pater? Where are you?"

"Right here." Her father's voice came from up above. "I can see the lighthouse."

"Flavia," said a woman's voice. "Let go. You can't carry them all. You're only a girl."

"Mater?" cried Flavia. "Oh, Mater, I've missed you so much."

"Shhh!" Flavia felt a cool hand on her hot forehead. "Let go, Flavia. The world will continue and the gods will have their way."

"Won't everyone die if I let go?" said Flavia.

"Yes. Eventually. But you can't prevent it. Let go, Flavia."

"I'm frightened."'

"Don't be frightened. Just let go. It will be all right."

So Flavia let the shield fall and everyone tumbled onto the ground. Some of them were laughing and some of them were angry. But Flavia didn't care.

She felt lighter than she had ever felt before, and freer.

"Oh Mater!" she sobbed. "Promise you won't leave me again?"

"Shhh! I can't promise that. But I'm here now."

Flavia felt her mother's arms around her—firm but soft—and she pressed her face against the smooth neck and wept.

And presently she slept.

# SCROLL XXVI

"Oh," Flavia groaned. "Where am I?"

"Father! She's awake!" It was Jonathan's voice.

"Ugh!" said Flavia. "My mouth feels like something crawled in and died."

"I know exactly what you mean," said Jonathan. "And I only had the fever for two days." She felt his firm hand under her neck and tasted cool water on her tongue.

When she had drunk her fill, Flavia rested her head back on the pillow and looked around. She was in her bedroom. From the pattern of bright diamonds on her bedroom wall, she guessed it was mid-morning.

"What time is it?" She frowned.

"About the third hour," said Jonathan. He was sitting on the side of her bed with a copper beaker of cool water. "And in case you're interested, today's the Sabbath."

"Saturn's day? But how can it be? Isn't today Mercury's day?"

Doctor Mordecai came into the room, drying his hands on a linen towel. His face looked thin and pale under the dark turban and there were shadows under his eyes.

"Doctor Mordecai, what happened?" said Flavia. "The last thing I remembered I was waiting by the road for . . . How did I get back here?"

"You'll never guess who found you," said Jonathan.

"Pater? Was it Pater?"

"No," said Mordecai. "We found him upstairs in his bedroom. Everyone in your house has had the fever. All except for Nubia. You were lucky we found you."

"Mater!" Flavia tried to sit up. Then she let her head fall back on the pillow. A hot tear trickled from the corner of her eye. "I dreamed Mater was alive. She was looking after me."

Jonathan and his father exchanged glances.

"No," said Jonathan. "It was Cartilia. She stayed with you day and night for three days. She and Nubia tended you and your father and Aristo. Alma's better now. Caudex, too. Nubia's sleeping in the spare room, and Cartilia went home a few hours ago."

"Oh," said Flavia. "I thought it was Mater." Her cheeks were wet and she turned to look at him. "It was Cartilia? After all I've done to her?"

Jonathan nodded.

"It's thanks to her your father is alive," said Mordecai. "She called me out two nights ago when his fever was at its worst. If I hadn't treated him. . . ."

"Is Pater . . . ?"

"He'll be fine," said Mordecai. "I've just been with him. He's awake and he's having some broth. Alma's with him. I'm just about to check on Aristo."

As Mordecai went out, Scuto tapped into the room and wandered over to Flavia.

"Oh, Scuto," said Flavia, hugging his furry neck. "I've missed you. Did you find me?"

"No," said Jonathan with a grin. "It was the last person you'd expect."

Flavia looked at him. "Was it Felix?" she whispered.

Jonathan sighed and rolled his eyes. "No, Flavia. It wasn't Felix."

"Give me a clue then."

"Who practically lives out in the woods?"

Flavia thought for a moment. Then her eyes lit up: "Diana?"

Jonathan nodded. "Diana."

Although the Saturnalia was officially over, Flavia's father had allowed them to recline for dinner on the pretext that they were still weak from the fever.

"Next week you're back at the table like proper Roman children," he'd told them. "But for the next few days I'll allow you to recline."

"Those oysters were delicious!" said Flavia. "Who sent them?"

"Pliny again," laughed her father. "He heard we were all at the gates of Hades and he sent us four dozen, on ice if you can believe that! We still have a dozen if you want more."

"No thanks," said Flavia. "I think my stomach shrank while I was ill. Lupus, do you want another one?"

Lupus shook his head, then uttered a deep, textured burp.

"Thank you for that compliment, Lupus," said Captain Geminus, and everyone laughed.

Jonathan tried his best to burp but could only manage a small one.

Flavia tried, too, without success, but Cartilia managed a rich yet ladylike belch.

Lupus clapped and Jonathan raised his eyebrows in admiration.

"Cartilia!" said Marcus, laughing, then he leaned forward and kissed her quickly on the cheek.

"Marcus!" she said with a blush. "Not in public."

"It's not public. It's my home. I'm the paterfamilias and I'll do as I like. Any objections?" He looked around, his gray eyes bright.

"No, Pater!" said Flavia with a smile. She was glad to see him happy again.

"I'm already feeling the effects of those oysters," said Aristo. "I feel like a new man. Nubia, shall we play some music?"

Nubia nodded.

"Oh yes," said Flavia. "I need to hear music so badly. Did you bring your barbiton, Jonathan?"

"Of course!" He smiled and pulled it out from beneath the couch.

Lupus already had his drums ready.

Flavia slipped off the couch and ran upstairs. A moment later she came back into the dining room. She went to Cartilia and solemnly held out her tambourine.

"Here, Cartilia," she said. "I'd like you to play it."

"Thank you, Flavia!" Cartilia's eyes were moist. "Thank you very much."

Flavia sighed and looked at her father. He gave her the merest nod, and a smile. Flavia went back to the couch and stretched out beside Nubia. She still felt weak.

Aristo was tuning his lyre. He hadn't played it in several days.

Then he looked at Nubia and she looked back at him and they began to play together.

Presently Jonathan came in on his barbiton. Lupus was drumming but he'd found some ankle bells and wore them on his right wrist. They made a sparkling noise as he beat the drum. Cartilia's tambourine was perfect. It was as if she'd practiced with the others for years.

Flavia smiled. They were playing "Slave Song."

As they played, she remembered another dining room in another time and place. And suddenly she felt his presence. As real as if he was reclining on the couch beside her.

He wasn't, of course, but when she closed her eyes she saw his face with its amused half-smile and beautiful dark eyes.

He hadn't come to save her. He probably hadn't even thought about her more than once or twice in the past few months. She knew it now with a terrible certainty. She knew the object of her passion was only a phantom.

The music and his image brought a surge of emotion from her so strong that she had to bite her lip to stop the tears coming.

"No," she whispered, digging her fingernails into her palms. "No, no, NO!" And once again she slipped off the couch and ran upstairs.


"Flavia. Are you all right?"

Flavia lifted her head to see Cartilia standing at the door.

"Flavia," said Cartilia. "What's the matter? You look perfectly miserable."

"You wouldn't understand. . . ." Flavia dropped her head back onto the pillow.

The bed creaked a little as Cartilia sat on the edge of it. "I might."

Flavia buried her face in the damp pillow. After a moment she said in a muffled voice: "I'm hopelessly in love."

There was a pause.

"Tell me about him."

Flavia slowly turned and looked up. Cartilia wasn't mocking; her expression was grave.

"He's married," said Flavia. That should wipe the understanding look off Cartilia's face.

But it didn't.

"It's a shame he's married," said Cartilia, "but we can't always choose whom we fall in love with, can we?"

Flavia shook her head. "And he's very old," she added.

"How old?"

"As old as Pater. Older maybe."

"Lots of women marry older men. My sister in Bononia married a man twenty years her senior."

"She did?" Flavia sniffed, then wiped her nose on her finger.

Cartilia nodded. "And they have a very happy marriage." She gently brushed a strand of hair away from Flavia's forehead. "Tell me about this man," she said. "Why do you love him?"

145

Flavia had been longing to talk to someone about him. And Cartilia was listening. So she pushed her pillow against the wall and sat up in bed.

"I met him three months ago," she said shyly. "After the volcano exploded. He's not the most handsome man I've ever seen, but his eyes. The way he looks at you. And I love his voice and the way his hair smells and he's very important and everybody respects him but when he looks at me he really looks at me and I just melt inside. And I love him so much," her chin began to tremble, "but he doesn't even . . ." She was crying again.

"Good heavens," said Cartilia. "He sounds like an extraordinary man. May I ask his name?"

"Felix. He lives in Surrentum and he's—"

"What?" interrupted Cartilia. "Not Publius Pollius Felix?"

Flavia's stomach flipped when Cartilia said his name. She nodded.

Cartilia burst out laughing.

Flavia felt fresh tears well up.

"I'm sorry," said Cartilia. "I shouldn't have laughed. But I suppose you know that half the women in Campania are in love with him."

"They are?"

Cartilia nodded. "I've never met him, but . . ." She smiled down at Flavia and then her eyes opened wide as Flavia shyly took her Felix doll out from under the pillow.

"Is this him?" said Cartilia, carefully taking the small wooden figure.

Flavia nodded. "Jonathan and Lupus gave it to me for the Saturnalia. It looks just like him."

"He's very handsome. I can see why you love him. But Flavia?"

"Yes?"

Cartilia held up the Felix doll. "Isn't he a bit short for you?"

Flavia looked at Cartilia, whose eyes were wide and solemn.

146

Then they both burst out laughing. They laughed for a long time and presently Cartilia said,

"Do you feel better now that you've told me and we've laughed about it?"

Flavia nodded and smiled.

"Will you still think about him all the time?"

"Maybe not. . . ." But even as Flavia said it a lump rose in her throat and her heart felt too tight. She felt the tears well up again.

"Yes," she whispered. "I'm still going to think about him."

"Flavia, you know the story of Pygmalion, don't you?"

"Of course. He was an artist and he made an ivory statue of the perfect woman. And then he fell in love with the statue and prayed to Venus and asked her to make the statue real."

Cartilia took the Felix doll and gazed at its face. "We are all a bit like Pygmalion," she said. "We create our perfect mate."

"I don't understand." Flavia hugged her legs and rested her chin on her blanketed knees.

"Pygmalion carved his ideal woman in his studio. We women carve the ideal man in our hearts." Cartilia held up the Felix doll. "We find someone whose appearance pleases us and then we create a man in their likeness and place him in our dreams. We build a whole life. One scene on another. And because we build them in our dreams, they're perfect. So we fall hopelessly in love. But we love a phantom. An image."

"Yes," said Flavia. "That's exactly what I was thinking."

"You don't really know anything about Felix, do you?"

"Not really," said Flavia. "But I still love him so much I could die."

Cartilia sighed. "You know what you have, don't you Flavia? You have the bite of the tarantula."

"I don't think I've been bitten by one of those," said Flavia. "Unless it was at night while I was asleep."

"No." Cartilia smiled. "The wise women of Calabria, that's where my mother comes from . . . they believe that the awakening

147

of first love is the most passionate love of our lives. This first love is so fierce that they call it the Tarantula's Bite."

"Is it a bit like Cupid's arrow?" said Flavia.

"Exactly," said Cartilia. "That's exactly it. We just call it something else in Calabria."

"Pater doesn't believe I'm in love. He says that I'm still just a child and it's only a 'girlish infatuation.'"

"I think he's wrong," said Cartilia. "Girls your age, on the cusp of womanhood, feel awakening love more acutely than at any other time in their lives. Your love is very strong. But Flavia," she said, gently tipping Flavia's chin up and gazing into her eyes, "you do know it can never be, don't you?"

Flavia nodded. "But I love him so much. The longing won't go away. I've tried but I can't stop thinking about him."

"If I told you I know a way to cure the Tarantula's Bite," said Cartilia, "would you be interested? Do you want to be cured of your longing for him?"

Flavia thought about it. Part of her loved being in love. But mostly it hurt too much. She looked up into Cartilia's warm brown eyes.

"Yes," she said. "I want to stop thinking about him all the time. I just want to be normal me again and think about puzzles and mysteries and stories. Is there a cure?"

"Yes," said Cartilia. "There is. It's a dance called the Little Tarantula. If you like, I will teach it to you."

"Yes," said Flavia. "Please teach me."

"Me, too," said Nubia, stepping shyly into the room. "I would like to dance the Little Tarantula, too. I also have the spider bite."

# SCROLL XXVII

Nubia was trembling. At last she had told someone.

"You're in love, too?" cried Flavia.

Nubia nodded.

"Who is it?" said Flavia.

"I think I know," said Cartilia softly. "You love Aristo, don't you?"

Nubia dropped her head and nodded again.

"How did you know that?" Flavia stared at Cartilia. "Even I didn't know."

Cartilia beckoned Nubia, who came to sit beside her on Flavia's bed.

"I can tell by the way they play music together," said Cartilia, putting her arm around Nubia's shoulder.

Presently she spoke.

"Usually we dance the Little Tarantula at the end of May, during the festival of Dionysus. But tomorrow night there is a full moon. We'll dance in the Grove of Diana."

"Outside the city walls?" gasped Flavia. "But what about the spirits of the dead?"

"They won't bother us," said Cartilia. "The god Dionysus will protect us."

"It will be cold and dark," Nubia shivered.

"Yes," said Cartilia. "At first. But as long as the weather stays dry, we'll be fine." She squeezed Nubia's shoulder and laughed. "You look at me reproachfully with those big golden eyes, but I promise you won't be cold. The dance will heat your blood."

In the end there were ten of them.

Somehow, the young women of Ostia heard about the Little Tarantula and they slipped out of their homes and gathered at the house on Green Fountain Street. Alma let them in.

The men—Flavia's father, Aristo, and Caudex—retreated to their rooms. If the sound of feminine chatter disturbed them, they gave no sign of it.

The young women drank hot spiced wine and gossiped and warmed their hands around the brazier in the triclinium. At last, when the moon's silver disc was at its zenith, they opened the back door and slipped out into the night.

Each one held a smoking torch and when they reached the grove they planted a circle of fire flowers.

Cartilia showed Flavia and Nubia how to hold the tambourine, not in the left hand, but in the right. She showed them how to keep the wrist and elbow moving but the forearm strong. She showed them how to let the emotion flow down the legs to the soles of the feet and through the arms to the fingertips.

"There will come a moment," she said, "when your feet will hurt, your forearms ache, your fingers might even bleed. You must keep playing; that is the point at which the god takes you and burns the passion from you."

They nodded. Cartilia slowly started to beat her own tambourine and to sing. The women joined her and shook their tambourines, or castanets, or clapped their hands. Some were peasants and a few were highborn. Most were in their teens. Cartilia, at twenty-four, was the oldest.

Presently they settled into a rhythm and they began to dance.

At first Flavia felt foolish, self-conscious. What was she doing, dancing in the woods on a cold winter's night with strange women around her? But the beat was strong and soon the music filled her head.

Nubia was dancing the Little Tarantula as if she had known it from birth. Cartilia was lost in the music, too. Her beautiful dark hair—the color of sesame oil—swung about her face. Flavia's forearms ached and her feet hurt, but the driving beat would not let her rest.

And then a figure appeared out of the darkness and joined them. It was Diana. She did not have a tambourine but she sang in a high, sweet voice and she begged the god to free her of her obsession.

It was then that the music took Flavia. Like a wave, it lifted her up and carried her and she was no longer tired. She closed her eyes and his face was there, so she danced out her yearning and her regret, her anger and her tenderness, her love and her hate.

Once, she opened her eyes and thought she saw him standing in the deep shadows outside the torchlight. But she realized that if it was not her imagination, it must be the god Dionysus, watching his women with approval.

Flavia lost all sense of time. Above her the stars blazed in the cold black sky and it seemed to her that she saw their shining paths, like snail silver, arc across the sky. As she danced, his beautiful face faded and presently, when she closed her eyes, she saw only the red-brown flicker of the torches through her eyelids.

And by dawn, when the watery sun had diluted the dark wine of night, Flavia knew that at last she was free of love's poison.

# SCROLL XXVIII

Tired but happy, with disheveled hair and bloodshot eyes, the group of women went chattering through the Laurentum Gate, laughing at the expression on the watchmen's faces. They had their arms around each other's waists. Flavia walked between Nubia and Cartilia, whose other arm encircled her sister Diana.

They went to the Baths of Minerva as the doors were opening and they paid their coin. They took off their sweat-stained clothes and sank gratefully into the myrtle-scented hot plunge. There, they let the steaming water soak away any remnants of passion, bitterness, jealousy, and regret.

Back at Green Fountain Street, Flavia and Nubia slept all that day and through the following night. And when Flavia awoke from a sweet dreamless sleep, she rose and dressed and took her Felix doll to the Temple of Venus.

And there she laid his image down on the altar.

"Venus," she prayed. "I give you all my dreams of love and marriage and romance. I lay them on your altar." Flavia bowed her head for a moment. The verse of a song Miriam often sang came into her head: "By the gazelles, O daughters of Jerusalem, do not awaken or arouse love until it so desires."

Flavia looked up at the statue of Venus. The marble goddess—caught in the act of slipping on her sandal—looked back at her in surprise.

"Venus," whispered Flavia. "Please do not arouse or awaken love in me until I'm ready."

And it seemed to her, though it may have been a trick of the light, that the goddess smiled kindly.

That evening, after dinner, Cartilia came up to the girls' room to tuck them into bed.

After she had kissed Nubia's forehead she came and perched on Flavia's bed. Scuto thumped his tail and Cartilia scratched him behind the ear.

"I should have known you weren't evil," said Flavia, "because Scuto likes you."

"Why did you think I was evil?" asked Cartilia, with a laugh.

"I thought you were the one who criticized Pater for letting me be too independent," said Flavia. "I thought it was your idea to marry me off."

"Not at all," said Cartilia. "That was your father's patron Cordius. He strongly disapproves of independence in women. That's why I told him my husband had died. If Cordius had found out that my husband divorced me for being too independent . . . Well, he never would have introduced me to your father. So my family all agreed to say I was a widow. It was foolish. I see that now. But I wanted to meet your father very badly."

"Tell me again about the first time you saw him?"

"The very first time was over half a year ago. He was walking along the docks, talking to one of his sailors. The wind was in his hair and he was laughing and I remember thinking to myself: Perhaps it's time I remarry. I asked my father to find out about him. Pater said he was a widower with one daughter and that his patron was Cordius, a very conservative man."

"And then what?"

"He went away before I could meet him, but then he came back, as if from the dead. I thought I'd better seize the day."

"*Carpe diem!*" laughed Flavia.

153

"Exactly. Pater invited Cordius to dinner and he invited us back. That was when I met your father." She smiled. "We got on very well. We laugh at the same things. He's kind and thoughtful. And he's honest."

"So you weren't like Pygmalion. You didn't make him into your dream man. You didn't just fall in love with the way he looks."

Cartilia flushed slightly. "Well," she said. "I do have to admit I find him very attractive. Plus, he still has all his teeth."

Flavia giggled and reached up to touch one of Cartilia's silver earrings; it was a pendant shaped like a tiny club of Hercules.

Then she remembered something: "But someone said it was your fault your husband died."

"Who?"

"Diomedes, the priest of Mithras. Actually I think his exact words were 'He's not with us anymore and it's her fault.'"

"Oh, that silly cult. I talked Postumus out of attending. All they wanted was his money."

"But later he divorced you because you were too independent, and because you couldn't have children?"

Cartilia nodded. "But he's just divorced his second wife for the same reason. So the fault may not be mine. As for my being too independent," she dropped her voice to a whisper. "I think your father likes independent women. The key is being subtle about it. And gracious. If you are those things I don't think he'll mind your independence."

"Cartilia?" Flavia stopped toying with her earring.

"Yes?"

"Tomorrow is a special day in Miriam's wedding preparation. They call it the day of henna. Jonathan says all the women in her family go and they tell stories and play music while they put henna designs on Miriam's hands and feet. It's at her aunt's house and she's invited Nubia and me and . . . will you come with us? We're going about midday."

"Oh, Flavia! I'd love to. Thank you so much for asking me." Cartilia bent down and kissed Flavia's forehead and gave her a hug.

Presently she stood up and started out of the room. Then she stopped and turned and Flavia saw her slender silhouette against the pale rectangle of the doorway.

"Flavia. I know it's always hard to share a parent, especially if you're an only child. Thank you for sharing your father with me. I promise I'll make him very happy. And I'll try to make you happy, too."

"I know," said Flavia, and she smiled. "Good night, Cartilia."

Something was wrong.

Flavia's step quickened as she and Nubia approached Cartilia's house. The front door was wide open and Vibia stood weeping before a bald man in a toga. He was shaking his head and as they drew closer they saw that Vibia was not wearing her wig.

"Oh, Flavia!" Vibia turned her tear-stained face toward the two girls. "Tell your father to make an offering to the gods and come quickly. Cartilia and Diana, and my husband . . . They've all come down with fever and the doctor says it's very grave."

# SCROLL XXIX

Doctor Mordecai confirmed what the Greek doctor had said.

"This second wave of fever is worse than the first," he said grimly. "I've lost half a dozen patients in the last two days, four of them little children. I've treated Poplicola and his daughters. The best thing you can do now is make sure they drink plenty of broth and keep them covered. They need to sweat out the evil humors."

Flavia and Nubia and Marcus stayed at Vibia's for three days. They helped her tend Cartilia and Diana, while she nursed her husband.

Presently Diana recovered and was able to sit up and take some solid food. But Cartilia's father died, and she herself slipped deeper into a fevered sleep. Now she could not even drink the broth. Her lips were blue and sometimes she fought for breath.

Once, when Flavia was sitting with her, she called out names in her delirium. First she cried out for her mother, then she called the name Marcus.

Flavia took Cartilia's hands and said, "He'll be back soon, Cartilia. He's just tired because he sat up with you all last night. He's having a little rest." She felt the tears coming. "Don't die, Cartilia," she pleaded. "Please get better. Pater loves you very much."

Cartilia turned her head and though her eyes didn't open she seemed calmer.

Flavia pressed a cool cloth to her forehead and said, "If you get better you can teach me more dances. And other things. Girl things." Flavia tried to make her voice bright but the tears were spilling out now. "Cartilia, I'm so sorry I was horrible to you. Please don't die. Pater needs you. And . . . I need you, too."

Flavia had just finished dressing when she heard the front door close. She hurried downstairs to find her father in the atrium, standing before the lararium. He still wore his cloak and his boots were muddy. He turned as he heard her step, and the look of bleak despair on his face told her everything: Cartilia was dead.

"Oh, Pater!" she cried, and ran to him. They held each other tightly and wept, standing there in the cold atrium before the household shrine.

Presently Flavia lifted her tear-streaked face.

"Pater, I know nothing will make it better but I promise I'll be good from now on. I'll never solve a mystery again and I'll stay inside and weave wool all day."

"No." He shook his head and looked at her through his tears. "I loved Cartilia because she had spirit and intelligence." He looked at the lararium. "Your mother had it, too, Flavia. A passion for life and a deep curiosity about the world. That's what I loved most about her. And about Cartilia." He looked at Flavia. "And that's what I love about you. Don't ever lose your hunger for knowledge."

"Then I can still be a detective?"

He nodded. "Yes, my little owl. Just . . . be sensible." He hugged her again and murmured into her hair. "You're all I have left now."

"I'll be sensible," said Flavia. She felt the soft wool of his tunic brush her cheek as she turned to look at the household shrine. The ancestral masks were shut away but she could see the painted figures representing the genius of the Geminus household, and the lares on either side. And the good-luck snake, coiling at the feet of Castor and Pollux and Vesta.

Flavia swallowed and stepped out of her father's arms so that she could look up into his face.

"Pater," she said. "Pater, I promise that I'll become a pious Roman matron and I'll have lots of children and then our family spirits won't be sad. And I promise . . ." Flavia took a deep breath. "Pater, I promise I'll marry whoever you think best."

The marriage took place seven days later.

The wedding procession was unlike any Ostia had ever seen before.

The young bride wore a white robe, a saffron yellow cloak, and a veil of bright orange. On her head was a garland of myrtle and winter violets. The town of Ostia was clothed in white, too, for it had snowed the night before. And as the bride emerged from the house after the wedding feast, the orange sun came out from its gauzy veil of high cloud. The snow sparkled like marble and the lion-head drains wore icicle beards.

A black-maned lion named Monobaz led the procession and a long-lashed camelopard took up the rear. The beautiful bride and her handsome groom rode in a chariot pulled by two donkeys. Although dusk was still an hour away, Jonathan and Lupus held smoking torches, while Flavia and Nubia scattered nuts to the people lining the streets. Hired musicians played double flutes, lyre, and tambourine, and the procession grew in number as they approached the Laurentum Gate.

Nubia wore her new fur cloak—a lion skin. It had been a gift from Mnason; the skin had belonged to one of his old lions. The combination of fur cloak and fur-lined boots meant that for the first time that winter Nubia felt warm outside the baths. When her nuts had all been scattered, she walked beside Monobaz and played her flute. The fresh clean scent of snow filled her head and she felt it scrunch under her leather boots.

As they passed under the arch of the Laurentum Gate, a new

song came to her. It was a song about starting over, when everything is pure and fresh and clean. Nubia decided to call it "Land of White."

The wedding procession passed through the gate and made its way along the Laurentum Road.

The hired musicians had been playing a jolly, rather shrill air on their double flutes and lyre. But Nubia's flute was playing a new song now and the hired flutes wavered. Lupus handed his smoking torch to Chamat and started beating his drum. Jonathan gave away his torch, too, and swung his barbiton to the front of his body. Together, they made the beat harder and stronger. The flute players struggled to keep up. Aristo hadn't brought his lyre, so he grabbed that of the lead musician who stared open-mouthed. Following his example, Flavia took the tambourine from another of the musicians.

It was a wonderful song that Flavia and her friends were playing now: a song of joyful hope with a driving beat.

As the procession moved on through the tombs, Flavia shook her tambourine and danced for Cartilia. She danced her regret for what would never be. For the laughter the two of them would never know. For the music Cartilia would never play. For the stories Cartilia would never hear. Or tell.

And when they left the tombs behind and moved between the woods and sea, toward the little house waiting in its snow-dusted vineyard, Flavia danced her joy of the family and friends who still remained. Her cheeks were wet but even as she wept, she smiled. Because although she grieved, she was alive. And that was a good thing.

Yes. It was very good to be alive.

# FINIS

# ARISTO'S SCROLL

Aeneas    (uh - **nee** - uss)
  Trojan son of the goddess Venus, he escaped from conquered
  Troy to have many adventures and finally settle near the
  future site of Rome

Aeneid    (uh - **nee** - id)
  Virgil's epic poem about Aeneas

Amphitryon    (am - fee - **try** - on)
  mortal father of Hercules (whose real father was supposedly
  Jupiter)

Apollodorus    (uh - pol - uh - **dor** - uss)
  Greek author who wrote an account of the Greek myths

Atalanta    (at - uh - **lan** - ta)
  beautiful princess who preferred hunting to marriage and for
  this reason set impossible tasks for her suitors

atrium    (**eh** - tree - um)
  the reception room in larger Roman homes, often with
  skylight and pool

Augeus    (ow - **gee** - uss)
  a mythical Greek king who neglected to clean his stables

barbiton    (**bar** - bi - ton)
  a kind of Greek bass lyre, but there is no evidence for a
  "Syrian barbiton"

Bononia    (bun - **own** - ee - uh)
    modern Bologna, a town in northeastern Italy
bulla    (**bull** - a)
    amulet of leather or metal worn by many freeborn children
Calabria    (kuh - **la** - bree - uh)
    the region of the "toe" of Italy
caldarium    (call - **dar** - ee - um)
    the hot plunge in a Roman baths; usually with a deep round
    pool of hot water
Campania    (kam - **pan** - yuh)
    the region around the Bay of Naples
Castor
    one of the famous twins of Greek mythology (Pollux is
    the other)
Cerberus    (**sur** - bur - uss)
    mythological three-headed dog who guards the gates of Hades
Ceres    (**sear** - eez)
    known as Demeter in Greek: the goddess of grain, crops
    and food
Cupid    (**kyoo** - pid)
    son of Venus and Vulcan, the winged boy god of love; those
    struck by his arrows fall in love
Decumanus Maximus    (deck - yoo - **man** - uss **max** - ee - mus)
    originally "a camp road," this was Ostia's main street
denarii    (den - **ar** - ee)
    more than one denarius, a silver coin. A denarius equals four
    sestercii.
Dionysus    (dye - oh - **nie** - suss)
    Greek god of vineyards, wine, and madness
divitiae    (div - **it** - ee - eye)
    the Latin word for "wealth"
Domitian    (duh - **mish** - an)
    the Emperor Titus's younger brother

duo

> Latin for "two"

equestrian  (uh - **kwes** - tree - un)

> literally "horseman," the social class of wealthy businessmen; to be a member of the equestrian class, you needed property worth at least 400,000 sestercii

Erymanthean  (air - im - **anth** - ee - un)

> region of the Erymanthos River in Arcadia, a part of central Greece

euge! (**oh**-gay)

> Latin exclamation: "hurray!"

Eurystheus  (yur - **riss** - thoos)

> mythological king for whom Hercules had to perform his tasks

Felix

> a wealthy patron and poet who lived in Surrentum in the late 1st century A.D.

forum  (**for** - um)

> ancient marketplace and civic center in Roman towns

frigidarium  (frig - id - **dar** - ee - um)

> the cold plunge in a Roman bath

fullers

> ancient laundry and clothmakers; they used human urine to bleach the wool

garum  (**gar** - um)

> sauce made of fish entrails, extremely popular for seasoning foods

Hades  (**hay** - deez)

> the Underworld where the spirits of the dead were believed to go

halva  (**hal** - vuh)

> a sweet made of honey and tahini (crushed sesame seeds), often with added pistachio nuts

Hebrew    (**hee** - brew)
>   holy language of the Old Testament, spoken by most Jews
>   in the 1st century, along with Aramaic and some Greek

Hercules    (**her** - kyoo - leez)
>   mythological hero; he had to complete twelve tasks to atone
>   for killing his family

Hesperides    (hes - **pair** - id - eez)
>   the daughters of Atlas, who lived in the remote west (modern
>   Morocco)

Hippomenes    (hip - **pom** - men - eez)
>   mythological hero who beat Atalanta at a race by throwing
>   golden apples

Ides    (eyedz)
>   the thirteenth day of most months in the Roman calendar
>   (including December); in March, July, October, and May the
>   Ides occur on the fifteenth day of the month

impluvium    (im - **ploo** - vee - um)
>   rectangular pool of water under the skylight (compluvium) in
>   the Roman atrium

Juno    (**jew** - no)
>   queen of the Roman gods, wife of the god Jupiter, and goddess
>   of childbirth

kohl    (kole)
>   dark powder used to darken eyelids or outline eyes

laconicum    (luh - **cone** - i - kum)
>   the hottest room in the Roman baths, the small laconicum
>   had dry heat

lararium    (lar - **ar** - ee - um)
>   household shrine, often a chest with a miniature temple on
>   top, sometimes a niche

lares    (**la**-raise)
>   household guardian spirits; it was the role of the paterfamilias
>   to keep them happy

Laurentum    (lore - **ent** - um)
   village on the coast of Italy a few miles south of Ostia
lustratio    (lus - **tra** - tee - oh)
   a ritual for purification of houses, ships, etc.
Minerva    (min - **nerve** - uh)
   known as Athena in Greek: the virgin goddess of wisdom
   and war
Mithras    (**mith** - rass)
   Persian god of light and truth, his cult—exclusively for men
   —spread throughout the Roman world after becoming
   popular with soldiers
mortarium    (more - **tar** - ee - um)
   rough flat bowl of clay or stone for grinding food
Nero    (**near** - oh)
   wicked emperor; built the Golden House after the great fire
   of Rome in A.D. 64
Ostia    (**oss** - tee - uh)
   the port of ancient Rome and hometown of Flavia Gemina
palla    (**pal** - uh)
   a woman's cloak, could also be wrapped round the waist or
   worn over the head
papyrus    (puh - **pie** - russ)
   the cheapest writing material, made of Egyptian reeds
paterfamilias    (**pa** - tare fa - **mill** - ee - us)
   father of the household, with absolute control over his
   children and slaves
peristyle    (**perry** - style)
   a columned walkway around an inner garden or courtyard
Pliny    (**plin** - ee)
   (the Elder) famous Roman author; died in the eruption of
   Vesuvius
   (the Younger) Pliny the Elder's nephew, who also became a
   famous author and statesman

poculum    (**pock** - yoo - lum)
>    a cup; here a liquid breakfast of spiced wine, milk, barley, and cheese

Pollux
>    one of the famous twins of Greek mythology (Castor is the other)

quattuor
>    Latin for "four"

quinque
>    Latin for "five"

Sabbath    (**sab** - uth)
>    The Jewish day of rest, counted from Friday evening to Saturday evening

Saturnalia    (sat - ur - **nail** - yuh)
>    five-day festival of Saturn, celebrated by the giving of gifts and relaxation of restrictions about gambling, slaves and masters often traded places for a day

scroll    (skrole)
>    a papyrus or parchment "book," unrolled from side to side as it was read

sestercii    (sess - **tur** - see)
>    more than one sestercius, a brass coin; four sestercii equal a denarius

sex
>    Latin for "six"

shalom    (shah - **lome**)
>    the Hebrew word for "peace"; can also mean "hello" or "good-bye"

sigillum    (**sig** - ill - um)
>    a doll of clay or wood, traditionally given on the Saturnalia; plural: sigilla

signet ring    (**sig** - net - ring)
>    ring with an image carved in it to be pressed into wax and used as a personal seal

stola    (**stole** - uh)
   a dress usually worn by Roman matrons (married women)
strigil    (**strig** - ill)
   a blunt-edged, curved tool for scraping off dead skin, oil, and
   dirt at the baths
stylus    (**stile** - us)
   a metal, wood, or ivory tool for writing on wax tablets
Stymphalian bird    (stim - **fay** - lee - an)
   a fierce mythical bird with claws and beak of bronze
sudatorium    (soo - da - **tor** - ee - um)
   the steam room in a Roman bath; often semicircular with
   marble benches
Surrentum    (sir - **ren** - tum)
   modern Sorrento, a pretty harbor town south of Vesuvius
tablinum    (ta - **blee** - num)
   the study in a Roman house
Tarantella    (tare - an - **tell** - uh)
   literally: the little tarantula, a dance to rid the body of poison
   or passion
tepidarium    (tep - id - **dar** - ee - um)
   the warm room in a Roman bath; usually for chatting and
   relaxing
Thetis    (**thet** - iss)
   a beautiful sea nymph, mother of Achilles and foster mother
   of Vulcan
Titus    (**tie** - tuss)
   the son of Vespasian and the emperor of Rome when this
   story takes place
toga    (**toe** - ga)
   a blanketlike outer garment, worn by freeborn men and
   boys
tres
   Latin for "three"

triclinium    (trick - **lin** - ee -um)
>   an ancient Roman dining room, usually with three couches to
>   recline on

tunic    (**tew** - nic)
>   a piece of clothing like a big T-shirt; children often wore a
>   long-sleeved tunic

unus
>   Latin for "one"

venefica    (ven - eh - **fick** - uh)
>   a sorceress who uses drugs, potions, and poisons

Vespasian    (vess - **pay** - zhun)
>   a Roman emperor who died six months before this story
>   begins

Vesta    (**vest** - uh)
>   known as Hestia in Greek: goddess of the home and hearth
>   (where the fire was)

Vesuvius    (vuh - soo - vee - yus)
>   the volcano near Naples which erupted on August 24 A.D. 79

vigiles    (**vig** - il - lays)
>   watchmen who guarded the town against robbery and fire

Virgil    (**vur** -jill)
>   a famous Latin poet who died about 60 years before this
>   story takes place; he wrote the *Aeneid*

wax tablet
>   a wax-covered rectangle of wood used for making notes

# THE LAST SCROLL

Long before people celebrated Christmas, the Romans celebrated a festival called the Saturnalia. It began as a one-day holiday, but by Flavia's time it had been extended to five days. Much later, when Christianity became the official religion of the Roman Empire, church leaders decided to celebrate the birth of Jesus at this time, so that people wouldn't be tempted to celebrate the "pagan" mid-winter festival. Therefore, many Christmas customs go back to the Saturnalia: decorating the house with green leaves, giving gifts, feasting and drinking. Even the riddles in Christmas crackers might go back to the practice of sending Saturnalia gifts with a short poem called an epigram.

The "little tarantula" dance is real. Today it is called the Tarantella, and people still dance it in parts of Italy. Some believe it began as a cure for the first passion of adolescent girls. We are not sure of its origins, but we do know that as far back as Greek times groups of women sometimes used to go into the woods and dance themselves into a trancelike state.

Ostia was and is a real place. You can visit its ruins today. The characters in this story are made up, but who knows? People just like them might once have lived—and loved—in Ostia.

*The Roman Mysteries*

## THE THIEVES OF OSTIA

The year is A.D. 79. The place is Ostia, the port of Rome. Flavia Gemina, a Roman sea captain's daughter, is about to embark on a thrilling adventure.

The theft of her father's signet ring leads her to three new friends—Jonathan the Jewish boy next door, Nubia the African slave girl, and Lupus, the mute beggar boy—who become her friends. Their investigations take them to the harbor, the forum, and the tombs of the dead, as they try to discover who is killing the dogs of Ostia, and why.

## THE SECRETS OF VESUVIUS

Flavia, Jonathan, Nubia, and Lupus sail to the Bay of Naples to spend the rest of the summer with Flavia's uncle who lives near Pompeii. They are soon absorbed in trying to solve a riddle that may lead them to a great treasure.

Meanwhile, tremors shake the ground, animals behave strangely, and people dream of impending doom. One of the worst natural disasters of all time is about to happen—the eruption of Mount Vesuvius. The four friends are in terrible danger!

## THE PIRATES OF POMPEII

A few days after Vesuvius erupts, the Roman world is reeling. Volcanic ash covers the land, sunsets are blood-red, and the sea gives up corpses of the dead. Hundreds of refugees from the cities around Vesuvius crowd into a makeshift camp.

When children from the camp begin to go missing, Flavia, Jonathan, Nubia and Lupus investigate a powerful and charismatic man known as the Patron. Their dangerous mission brings them up against pirates, slave dealers, and death.

## THE ASSASSINS OF ROME

Back in Ostia, the four friends are celebrating Jonathan's birthday when a visitor arrives to see Jonathan's father. Next day the visitor has disappeared, and so has Jonathan. His friends track him to Nero's Golden House in Rome, where a deadly assassin is at work.

The mystery is the darkest yet, as Flavia and her friends learn about the terrible destruction of Jerusalem, and its impact on Jonathan's family.

## THE DOLPHINS OF LAURENTUM

Flavia Gemina, the sea captain's daughter, and her friends Jonathan, Nubia, and Lupus, are at home in the port city of Ostia when the arrival of a ragged stranger shocks them all. To her horror, Flavia learns that her family is in danger of losing everything they own.

Events take Flavia and her companions to an opulent seaside villa south of Ostia and to the discovery of a sunken wreck and lost treasure. It seems to be the answer to Flavia's problems—but someone else is after the treasure, too. As the four friends try to recover it, they also uncover the terrible mystery of Lupus's past.